With grateful thanks to a patient husband and daughter.

NOCTURNE PROLOGUE

There is a new gown hanging in my room for tomorrow and he says I must always be well dressed because of his prestige and to show the public how happy we are. I will only be allowed to play solo with the Orchestra so that he can enjoy the limelight and always accompany me. Robert! Oh my Robert, I miss you so. My heart is breaking and I am so alone.

February 5th. This is the dreaded wedding morning, my day of doom. Forgive me my darling for what I am about to do. I have no choice. It is either this or lose our child.

February 12th. My life is more unbearable than I thought life could be. Every day is a burden with fresh horrors. My only consolation, that I have my

Robbie back with me. At first he fought and kicked me but I soon recovered him by gentle talk and loving. I dread to think what has happened to him. There are many bruises on his little body and he is very thin and frightened.

I had not thought Mr. Elliott would need or demand his conjugal rights. How naïve I was and how mistaken. When I refused him the first night he said,

"My dear Frances have you still not realized why you are in this position? You will give me a son because I require an heir and you will fulfil your wifely duties until this is accomplished."

Eleanor was then called to disrobe me while he calmly undressed.

CHAPTER ONE

The house was silent as strong, capable hands stroked the dark wood of the old cello and Frances pondered on the family mystery. Her thoughts nibbled around the Great, Grandmother to whom the instrument once belonged, the ancestor for whom she was said to be named. The beloved instrument passed from that other Frances in a direct line down the family to her and would go on to her daughter Charlie.

At that moment, Charlie breezed into the house on one of her flying dormitory visits, like a sudden shaft of brilliant sunlight. She lived in a flat in Denton, but often used her parental home in Hyde as a refuelling stop. If it were Thomas or Peter, Frances would have jumped up with embarrassment, but she didn't mind Charlie seeing her dreaming away the day while hugging the large piece of wood.

"Hi there Mum, wandering with the strings again?"
Dumping bags, coats and music case in the hall like a jumble heap, the whirlwind that was Charlie continued.

"Did you ever write to that magazine for information?"

"Mm, my letter's in the issue that arrived today. I don't expect any replies but it would be fun if there was just one. It would be a starting point."

"I suppose being in the magazine is the first step. I should be jumping up and down with impatience if it were me; I wish I had your calm."

With a hug and hurried kiss on her Mother's cheek, Charlie flew upstairs.

It was a standing joke that somebody in each generation was lumbered with the cello as a permanent boarder. It was referred to as Grandma's lodger, tolerated or loved, depending on the sentiments of the current custodian.

Frances was the only one of her family who appreciated the heirloom. Neither her elder sister Laura nor brother Ted was ever interested. Her mother Sarah always hated the thing and would have sold it years ago, if she dared. Frank, Frances' father inherited both the cello and the instrumental ability to play it. His mother Hannah Frances Banks, grandmother to Frances, taught him the basic skills, which he developed sufficiently to play in a theatre orchestra in his youth.

Frances, whose love of music passed like a living thread from her ancestor, learned to play the cello from her father because she pestered him to teach her almost as soon as she could walk. She remembered her Gran Hannah Frances playing when she was a very old lady, with Frances then a small child standing at her knee. Gran said to her then,

"Take care of this treasure child, it is very precious. My Mother earned her bread with it and one day, you will play too."

The picture of her white haired Gran stroking the cello all those years ago, just as she was doing now, floated through Fran's mind.

"Your Great Grandmother left part of herself with this cello, I feel it and you will feel it when you play. Put your hands here on the wood child and you will feel it talking to you."

The old lady placed the tiny hands of her granddaughter on the body of the cello to stroke the mellow old wood. Had it been imagination or did she really feel a tingle in her fingers all those years ago? Frances knew now, that the cello possessed its own magic because, after that she experienced the tingling sensation of some vital force, many times. Often in the early days of her learning to play, she felt the power of the cello. The bow in her uncertain hand and her small fingers seemed to be guided unerringly to the correct position on the strings, to produce some tune for which she had no music. Frances never admitted any of this to her husband

Leonard, or anybody else, for fear of ridicule. Their daughter Charlotte Frances, Charlie for short, wouldn't scoff because Frances suspected she too was aware of the energy and force contained in the instrument, which could be tapped by certain people.

Charlie taught music, was a brilliant player and performed as a cellist by invitation, if and when she chose. At twenty five Charlie was steeped in music, when not teaching or performing, she played with the Manchester city Orchestra in her leisure time.

Her brothers, Thomas and Peter were first to arrive in the family, both enjoyed music and passed through the stages of playing cornet, saxophone and guitar in their youth. If Frances told them of her communion with the cello, they would have her committed on the spot.

Fran continued to caress the old wood, murmuring to herself,

"I wish I could learn your story Great Grandmother, if only I'd thought to ask Dad or Gran when they were alive. They would perhaps have been able to tell me."

Frank died when his ship struck a mine in 1945, having gone all through the war on active service. He'd been home on leave and was probably on his last mission before demobilization. The shock of his death killed his mother Gran Hannah Frances, who suffered a heart attack the day after hearing the news and died the following week. Frances, a girl of eight, clung to the cello and her Mother was unable to get rid of it, because in the will Frank thoughtfully made before enlisting, he left it to his younger daughter.

When Frances asked her sister Laura if she knew anything about their ancestor or had seen any pictures of her, the reply was negative.

"I know nothing further back than Gran and never delve into things long gone. Too much to think about in the present! Why on earth do you want to go digging up the past?"

Brother Ted lived in Canada and owned a small cattle farm. When Frances wrote to him asking what he knew of their earlier relatives, his answer too was both unaware and unhelpful.

"Let me know what you discover Sis but I have too much to do at present to help your search."

Frances's mother Sara died in 1963. Father Frank's elder sister Charlotte and brother John both relocated below ground, so there was nobody able to tell Frances anything of the family

Frances was a newly joined member of the local branch of the Family History Society and the letter Charlie referred to was a request for help in the Member's page of their society magazine,

> Seeking information on Frances, talented cellist. Born around 1850 in Manchester area. Daughter Hannah Frances and son Charles.'

The magazine arrived that morning and Frances would have to wait at least a week before there could be any replies. Although she wasn't hopeful of a positive response, there was a feeling of excitement coiled inside her that perhaps there might be. At least the ball had started rolling.

The Society was running a trip for members to visit the Records Office in Kew Gardens, in London and Frances was joining them. There she hoped to discover some details about her Great Grandmother. For the hundredth time she wished she'd made a start on the trail of her ancestors many years ago, when there were people alive whom she could have asked. The desire to know more about that first Frances, her life and personality, became more insistent with passing time. How was her life connected with the cello and how did she come to own and play, what was in those days, an unusual instrument for a woman? There was no spare time for such a consuming hobby when she was working but since retiring from nursing, Frances was determined to at least try and find the story she was certain was waiting to be discovered.

Charlie bounded down the stairs, bursting through her Mother's reverie and jolting her back to the present.

"Will it be O.K to borrow the family heirloom for the concert this evening Mum? I thought I'd like to demonstrate the difference in tone, between the ancient and the modern instrument."

"That's a novel touch and even the least musical person will be able to discern a variation. You can use the cello whenever you like darling; the responsibility will be all yours when I no longer play, so we can surely share it now."

There was hesitation in her voice as she asked,

"Charlie?"

Charlotte, sorting through sheets of music but fully alert to the tone in her Mother's voice, chuckled

"Oh, I'm to be bequeathed this museum piece am I? What were you going to say?"

"Do you sometimes feel a vibration when you play it? I mean a kind of guidance?"

Charlie turned to her mother, her quick smile revealing a perfect set of pearly teeth and a small dimple at the side of her mouth,

"Of course I do and I know it happens to you. I'm quite sure too that the old girl chooses with whom she wants to live."

Frances smiled with relief at her daughter, who resembled no one else in the family. Her bright, bubbly personality concealed a deep perception and concern for others. Charlie considered herself fortunate in belonging to a caring family and to have so much and was always ready to give of herself. Frances marvelled again at her long thick mane of hair, a genuine dark chestnut with red / gold highlights. Her features were neat and regular and her eyes, that startling, violet blue that demands a second look. She was tall, slender and highly charged, bringing her restless energy and enthusiasm to whatever project consumed her at the time. Her open friendly face and nature drew people to her like a magnet. She was in total contrast to her Mother who was of stocky build and average height with dark colouring. Their external appearance being so different, it was a surprise to find their character and temperament so similar and in tune. Again Frances wished that her Father had lived long enough to know his grandchildren, instinctively aware to which child he would have been closest.

Charlie bundled out of the house in a assortment of cellos, music and stand, exuding perfume and verve, leaving behind a very empty space.

CHAPTER TWO

Tuesday morning brought the long forgotten time of five-o-clock and found Frances climbing aboard a special coach to begin the journey down to London. Clutched in her bag was her folder containing the little family information she'd gleaned so far, pads, pencils and magnifying glass. The birth certificate of her Father was already in her possession and from the age Gran Hannah was when she died, Frances could estimate her birth date. She dropped into the seat Amy was saving. Her friend was a mine of information, helping to launch her on the family search. Amy had been researching her roots intermittently, for several years when spare time allowed. It was she who urged Frances to join the Society and dragged her out at such an unearthly time on this misty March morning.

As Frances settled in for a long ride, Amy confided,

"I'm seeking information on my maternal side and am going to see if any of them left a Will. These can be really helpful with names of relatives. Also I'll see if they have Bishop's Transcripts. There's masses of material available when you know what to look for and it's fairly straightforward and well organized. The staff's very helpful too."

The coach travellers were friendly, society members and knew each other well from long association, and getting together at the monthly meetings. Uniting them was this burning, common purpose; to learn about their ancestors. The busy hum of conversation, mingled with the operational sounds of food parcels unfolding and the clink of mugs as flasks frothed out their fragrant contents.

"What's Leonard going to do with himself today Fran?" Amy inquired.

"You shouldn't need more than one guess. He packed some sandwiches last night and promised himself an early start to a day fishing. He was still a lump in the bed when I left so I've no idea what time early is. What about Denis?"

"He's going to do some work in the garden which probably means sitting and thinking about it if the sun shines."

Amy grinned as she passed Fran a steaming mug of coffee and screwed the lid back on the thermos.

"No sugar right?"

Frances nodded, taking a firm hold on the mug as she pulled down the table attached to the seat in front. Amy continued,

"Have you sorted out exactly what you're going to look for today? I've not been here before as the records were housed at the Records Office in Islington before the powers that be decided to move the whole caboose to Kew where the military records lived. It seemed sense to have them all in one place."

Amy took a long sip of her coffee before saying,

"If we know what information we want, the assistants will point us in the right direction."

Opening her folder, Frances showed her friend the sketchy family tree drawn there and the neatly written questions to which she was hoping to find answers.

"I want to find the birth date of my Gran Hannah Frances and maybe her marriage. If I can find those then I will know her maiden name, is that correct?"

"That's right, but if you don't already know her maiden name, you'll need to go for her marriage first. Not only will that tell you her maiden name and perhaps her age, it will also tell you the name of her father and his occupation. When you've found her birth and have the certificate, it tells you the place she was born with the names of both parents and her mother's maiden name."

"I think there was a brother Charles, who would be my Great Uncle, but he died years ago in the First World War I think, without marrying but I can't remember his name. Nobody seems to know anything about Charles; he was a bit of a mystery. I am so excited to think I may actually know more about Great Gran Frances when we board the coach tonight."

Amy told her,

"The registers start half way through 1837 so you could have a lot of searching to do love, but it's fun."

Frances scribbled a reminder on her notes while confiding,

"I wish I could find out more about the person she was. It will be wonderful to discover dates, places and names but what I would really love to know about, is HER. What kind of a person she was, her life and why the name Frances runs through the generations. It's really confusing."

Fran sipped her coffee thoughtfully before continuing,

"My Gran Hannah Frances told me her Mother earned her living with our cello and that's one reason we cherish it."

The coach was making good progress and the roads were not too busy at this time of the morning. Some of the group were snoozing but Fran was on a high and much too excited to miss anything and watched the dawn breaking over the countryside with appreciation. The interior of the coach was filled with rustlings and chatter and the smell of coffee floated around like heady perfume.

Amys voice roused Fran as she asked, "Have there been any replies to your request?"

"No and it's over a week now."

"Early days! People don't always devour their journal the first day like you and me." A dig in the ribs and a teasing grin accompanied the last remark and Frances received both with a shamed face. "

"Some people still have to work, so have less time for writing letters. You remember the days?"

Watching the mischievous expression in Amy's lovely dark eyes and the blonde hair framing her elfin face, she felt gratitude and affection for her friend.

"I'm being impatient, but after all these years, it's as though I'm being compelled to find out about her. Will I be able to buy certificates today do you think?"

"Mm. Not sure about that one. I heard somebody saying that you could order and pay for them and the office would post them on. Maybe it depends the time they are requested and the demand."

The coach disgorged the treasure seekers at Kew and they streamed around the lake and inside the beautiful old building. The record office had recently moved from Islington to Kew enabling family history records to be housed with Military archives.

Newcomers needed to have their photograph taken to put on membership cards before passing through the Security entrance. This didn't take long and Frances was soon joining Amy who already owned a 'passport'.

Amy was soon settled at one of the tables, wading through Index Fiche on Wills. Fiche is film full of information that is put into a special reading machine to search the content.

Very soon all the party, along with other visitors were settled at a film or fiche reader, or with books from the shelves. Fran was directed to the shelves housing the registrar's copies of Births, Marriages and Deaths and began to scan the lists of marriages. The records were held in massive tomes that weighed a ton and made her muscles scream. Each book held a quarter year for that part of the alphabet.

Frances had no idea when her Gran was married but from her research knew her Grandfather was Edward Banks. This was her own maiden name, although she couldn't remember him. She also knew her Father Frank was born on March 2nd 1908 and that there was an older sister and brother, both unfortunately deceased long ago.

Frances remembered her Aunt Charlotte as a very spinsterish lady who was particular about children saying please and thank you and wiping their feet. She reckoned that Uncle John, the eldest, could have been born around 1900 and began searching forwards from 1896, keeping a meticulous record of each quarter year she checked. Even with the facts she had, it was over an hour later that Frances found the entry for the marriage of an Edward Banks. She couldn't double check with the name of her Gran because she didn't know her maiden name. Taking a chance on it being the entry she was seeking, Frances asked the clerk if she could have a copy of the certificate. She was told this would be ready for her at two-o-clock, meanwhile she could proceed no further until she had that elusive maiden name.

Unsure what to do next, Frances used the valuable waiting time to acquire dates of births and deaths of the aunts and uncles she would need to fill the branches of her family tree. This occupied her until, surprised by the rumbling of her stomach, she found it past one-o-clock. Her search for Amy found her in the same room searching the Birth books. They went downstairs to the room designated for people with packed lunches, collecting their bags from the lockers provided. Here they ate their food and compared notes. Amy had found the Birth of one of her lost ancestors and was almost as excited as Frances when they went to collect the promised certificates.

With trembling fingers, Frances sat down to open the long sheet of stiff paper and read that her Grandfather Banks married Hannah Frances Elliott on March tenth, 1890, in Preston Lancashire.

Her father was recorded as William Elliott, a lawyer. The ages of both Edward and Hannah Frances were simply marked as full.

"Well that's not much help Amy." Frances felt acute disappointment, "Where do I go from here? It could take ages to search for the marriage of Gran's parents if I don't know Hannah's age when she married."

"Well there's always another way. Perhaps it would be better to look for the birth of your Gran Hannah now that you know her maiden name and you already know her age when she died."

Back at the shelves, Frances searched several years, when she reckoned Gran would be born until she located her birth in the third quarter of 1870. With this information she rushed to the desk and asked for the certificate just in time to get it that day. It would be ready at four o clock.

Now what should she look at? She couldn't just hang around with all this information around her. Elliott. Elliott. The name rang bells in her head until she remembered that was the name of Gran's brother Charles, Fran's great uncle. So she was on the right track. She could look up his birth to fill the precious time here. She found him less than a year after Gran.

'Wow.' muttered Fran,

'They didn't waste much time.'

Again Fran trotted off to the desk to order a copy of that certificate which would be posted to her.

Four o clock saw Fran again waiting to collect the next piece of the puzzle. Full of excitement she carried it to a table where she spread it out.

'1870, September 12th. at Brentwood House,
Park Road, Manchester.
Hannah Frances. Girl.
Father William Elliott. Lawyer.
Signature of informant. W Elliott father.
Mother Frances, late Brentwood.'

Fran almost shouted out a double 'wow'. There was so much to take in here. She found Amy over in the Wills section and they studied the information together. Amy considered the paper carefully

"So your Gt Gran Frances was married twice. First to a Mr. Brentwood. The next thing you need is that marriage certificate and you could look him up at our library on their marriage reels, otherwise you'll be waiting for the next trip to Kew eh!"

The homeward bound coach buzzed with the sound of conversation as people discussed the findings or failures of the day and exchanged views and opinions.

Fran pulled out her two certificates to gloat over,

"Gran Hannah's maiden name was Elliott and that reminded me that was the name of her soldier brother, my great uncle Charles, the name I couldn't remember. So, I now have to wait for the postman."

Fran heaved a huge sigh of resignation.

"Oops impatient again. It's going to be a long job to go a short way but a long journey back in years when you think about it."

Amy laughed,

"You're right there. You certainly do need patience Fran but it will be with you next week and it's something to look forward to."

"Mm, suppose you're right, I just want to know but I've been so lucky today to find all that. It was a real bonanza."

Fran carefully put away the precious certificates in her folder before asking,

"What are Bishop's Transcripts and where are they kept Amy? I heard one of the other searchers talking about them."

"They are held here in the archives and you can search them like the other records we've been looking at today. In past centuries, the vicar of each parish was required to make a copy of each entry in the Parish Register in his care, at every month end."

Amy searched her folder and showed Frances a copy of a scrawled entry of one of her family.

"So, for each entry in a Parish Register, whether a birth, death or marriage, an identical copy must be sent to his Bishop."

Fran studied the scrap of dirty paper closely before giving it back.

“These copies were often made in a hurry, perhaps being forgotten until the end of the month. Some were not identical to the original and most were in a hasty scrawl, at times almost illegible. Paper is a relatively recent invention and copies were made on any scrap of material the vicar could find, with no thought for us poor researchers decades and centuries later.”

Replacing the torn fragment, Amy put away her folder and settled herself for a long journey.

“Actually I believe events are still recorded and sent to the Bishop in the same way but maybe more legible or even electronically.”

With a huge sigh Fran leaned back in her seat,

“I’ve really enjoyed the activity and new experience today but, do you know,you know, I’m shattered.”

Relaxing back comfortably in her seat she mused,

‘I wonder when the cello comes into its own.’

Amy murmured agreement,

“I’m tired too but remember what time we were up this morning and we’ve been searching all day. Every little piece you glean adds to the picture.”

Amy shuffled back and placed a neck cushion in the gap behind her head to snuggle into before continuing,

"Like all our ancestors Fran, the closer you get to your Gran Hannah, the more mysterious she becomes and this is what keeps us searching and makes it so aggravating and such fun. The answer to one question creates another puzzle."

CHAPTER THREE

Frances' life was filled with a variety of activities and although she awaited the post each day, her time was fully occupied. Since his retirement Leonard worked two days each week and at least one morning when the weather was fine, Fran joined him for a walk into the country lanes. They took cartons of juice and a pack of sandwiches each, or stopped for a pub lunch somewhere. Fran also did some visiting of elderly people under the umbrella of the local branch of Red Cross. Her nursing experience gave her an interest in people and an understanding of their ailments and losses. The remainder of that week, the post yielded nothing more exciting than junk mail and a newsy letter from son Peter, hot from his computer.

On Monday morning, Fran greeted the postman eagerly, her steel-wool curls blowing in the wind, grey eyes sparkling with anticipation.

"'Mornin' Mrs. Smith. Is this the one you're waiting for? Doesn't look like a big win to me."

He passed the long buff envelope to Frances and exchanged views on the pleasant April morning before whistling away down the path.

Having written the address herself, there could be no doubt of the contents of the envelope. Tearing open the flap, she extracted the document and spread it on the kitchen table.

On July 10th. 1870, a birth was recorded in Manchester for a boy named Charles. Parents William and Frances Elliott, the address was the same as the other certificate but there was no additional information.

Fran decided to visit their local library to do a search for the marriage between Frances and this Mr Brentwood, her first husband. Shouting her intentions to Leonard, she set off on her bicycle. Thinking during her journey she decided to find the marriage to Mr Elliott first before the one to Mr Brentwood.

'One bit at a time she told herself.'

A section of the library was reserved for Family History and separated from the rest in a quiet area downstairs in the basement. This was a growing leisure hobby and new techniques were being introduced continually. It didn't house the amount of data as Kew, but was acquiring more each year. The internet was playing an increasing role here, as records were being digitalised and made available.

The marriages were still on a reel and an assistant set Fran on a reel machine and left her to forage for the year she estimated the marriage to be, ie nine months prior to her Gran Hannah's birth. She knew it could be a bit earlier or later and began searching from November because Gran Hannah was born on September 10th.

Fran hunted from October the previous year and found no trace of the marriage. Time having run out and a man waiting to use her machine, she booked another session for the following day and cycled round to Amy's house.

Over a cup of tea she told Amy of her quest,

"How could that happen? I know I didn't miss it so what?"

"Well maybe she was born prematurely? I suppose Frances' first husband must have died so you could look for a death too. Your Gran's birth must be recorded. It is a true fact. As you know every birth has to be registered by law."

Amy poured more tea and cut slices of her newly made strawberry sponge cake.

"If it were me I would go further forward to find that marriage. It must be there even if it is earlier or later than you suppose. It's not unheard of for a child to be born early in those days."

Fran bit into her cake while she pondered.

"You're right as usual. What a lot I have to learn but didn't have enough time this morning. Amy this cake is delicious, really light and fluffy. Must fly, Leonard wants to go out this afternoon. See you later in the week. Bye."

In front of her machine the following morning Fran searched forwards until she came upon a Marriage for William Elliott in the first quarter of 1870. Double checking with the name of Frances she found a match. Frances Brentwood married William Elliott in the first quarter of 1870 and her Gran Hannah Frances was born on Sept.12th. 1870 the same year. So she was a premature baby.

'Well I never." Mused Fran, 'That's a lot earlier than I would have thought. I still have time to search for her first marriage.'

Looking back several years she found the marriage for a Robert Brentwood in the first quarter of 1865. The helpful librarian gave her an address where she could obtain the certificates for a fixed charge and forms to fill in details.

On arriving home she rang Amy to tell her.

"Hi Amy, had a successful morning and didn't call as I thought you might think I'd come for more of that lovely cake. As you thought, Gran was born much earlier than I thought. I'll post off the request form today so may have more news by next week. I hope."

"Cake all gone I'm afraid. It's a waste of time baking at this house; it simply disappears in tuck boxes. Let me know when the post arrives I'll call in. Bye now."

A few days later Fran was cleaning windows when their well-known local postman crunched up the path waving some mail.

"More fan mail for you Mrs Smith, there's no end to your fame."

Handing over the pile of post he chuckled off down the path, his heavy boots clanking on the concrete like hammer blows.

In amongst Leonard's mail were two familiar looking buff envelopes. Cutting open the first she extracted a certificate for the marriage of Robert Brentwood a bachelor aged thirty, who married Frances Brown, a spinster aged eighteen years in Manchester on March 17th. 1865.

Fran rang Amy,

"Good morning. Do you want to come over for coffee around ten?"

"Aha, I bet you've something to show me."

"Just wait and see," teased Frances.

After putting on the kettle and setting cups for coffee Fran opened the second envelope, she scanned the certificate for the marriage of her Gt

Gran Frances to William Elliott. This confirmed her name as Brentwood and the date just seven months prior to Gran Hannah's birth.

While enjoying her coffee and poring over the certificate, Amy spotted a detail Frances missed on the first marriage.

"I see the father of your Gt. Gran Frances was a Reverend gentleman."

"Where? Where does it say that?" asked an incredulous Frances.

"Here look, end column. Where it says 'name of father and occupation'. It says Robert Brown Vicar. This is really exciting Fran. So your next step is to look to see if Robert Brentwood died soon after their marriage."

Fran refilled their coffee cups and pushed the biscuits across the table, saying thoughtfully,

"Mmm. I can't help feeling there is a story here and wishing I could find what it is. I suppose we'll never know all of that."

"Just an idea Fran, but how about placing an ad. In a National Magazine, something like the Family Tree. You may have to pay but it goes all over the country not like our little local mag. You're more likely to catch a fish."

"I've never heard of that one but I'm willing to give anything a try that will flush out information and I can give more facts now. For instance I know she was Frances Brown."

Weeks passed after Frances placed her ad. In the National magazine and hope of anything positive arising from it was slowly fading. There were two red herrings but the writers were so obviously unconnected that after replying with thanks, their letters were filed away. Amy told her to save everything as any information could link in at some stage.

CHAPTER FOUR

Fran was excited about the imminent birth of their first grandchild and preparing to travel to visit when the news came of the arrival. In her opinion eldest son Thomas and his wife Janet were the most unlikely couple. Janet's occupation as a social worker continued almost until her due date and Fran was secretly appalled at her lack of preparation and slap happy ways. However, she was touched when Janet asked her if she could spare a few days to stay with them until she felt more sure of herself. Janet's parents immigrated to Australia with younger siblings and there was no family support nearby.

So, it was arranged that when Thomas brought home his wife and baby, Frances would stay a week with them in Lincoln. After that Thomas could have a week of his holidays to give more assistance.

When the message came that Leonard and she were now grandparents to a healthy baby girl Fran was already packed and ready to catch the train.

Despite her misgivings, Frances enjoyed this week with her eldest son and his family. Janet was very much the new mother, inexperienced and vulnerable. She appealed to the maternal instinct in Frances and after one or two sessions of tears and despair, Janet came to trust the calm sense and dependability of her mother in law. As Fran watched her sitting comfortably with an absorbed and faraway expression on her face she knew the mothering instinct had kicked in. Her black hair pushed back from her face and her warm brown eyes gazing down at her baby intently suckling were a picture to stay in the mind. Gradually, the regimen of feeding was greeted with joy instead of dread.

Thomas was a Doctor in General Practice and home for a couple of hours each day. He took a refresher course on routine and orderliness by watching his mother's efficient routine. Whether this could be maintained after her departure, Frances doubted.

When his mother took yet another load of washing from the machine and went to hang them out in the sunny breeze. Thomas followed her.

"You know Thomas, if you could afford some help in the house, even for two hours a week, it would be a great start for Janet. The early weeks are important for a new mother's well-being and everything is so strange for her."

"I think we could manage a few hours help and there's a woman just down the road who might come in one or two mornings,"

"That would be great Thomas. If we lived nearer, there would be no problem dear; I could pop in for an hour every morning." Fran was pegging out a tiny baby-grow as she talked,

"Sitting to feed and care for a young baby takes so many hours out of the day, there's no time left for chores and that causes stress."

Frances learned to love her daughter in law and appreciate that, in spite of her disorderliness and lack of method, Janet had a warm, loving nature. She would enjoy her baby even if the laundry piled up around her and there were no clean clothes to wear or pots to use.

Leonard rang most evenings to keep Frances informed of things at home and she knew there was a letter awaiting her attention. It was a wrench leaving her baby granddaughter, whose name promised to be Bethany. Janet and she knew each other much better now and were far closer than before. Perhaps the difference was that she'd been the visitor in their home instead of the other way around. The two of them also shared some fun and laughter which cemented the bond. There was genuine sadness on all sides when goodbyes were said.

"I shall be back soon, let me know when you go for your check up and I'll come and stay over. You can save up your ironing and I'll do you a big bake. The good weather is coming so you can all get outside a bit more."

Leonard was touchingly pleased to see her home safely and put a cup of tea in her hand almost before she was inside the door. A tall man of lean build, his ruddy complexion told of an active outdoor life. He'd managed his life in Fran's absence by using the meals she'd prepared and put in the freezer or by eating out.

There were several letters requiring attention, but the envelope riveting her eyes bore a strange handwriting. Forcing down her impatience she tried to respond to what Leonard was telling her; the events in his week and the doings of their neighbours seemed trivial when her fingers were itching to open the strange envelope with the Oldham postmark.

CHAPTER FIVE

As soon as good manners allowed, Frances took out the short handwritten missive and read,

Dear Mrs. Smith,

I am a direct descendant of a Frances Brown who married Robert Brentwood and later a William Elliott. I believe this to be the person you are seeking. To facilitate an early meeting to discuss this, I enclose my telephone number and look forward to hearing from you at your earliest opportunity.

Yours sincerely,

Robert Francis Brentwood.

Leonard never showed more than a mild interest in her family quest, he was simply pleased she'd discovered such an absorbing hobby.

When she read aloud the letter he said,

"Why not invite him over here, we could give him lunch and presumably he has a wife. Fancy another part of the family living so near and being unaware of their existence. We could maybe offload Gt. Gran's heirloom." He chuckled as he checked the postmark for a date,

“That letter’s been here several days love; you should give him a ring now. Today being Sunday, he’s likely to be in.”

Leonard’s aesthetic face expressed the animation usually reserved for politics, the swings of the stock exchange or the feel of a fishing rod in his hands. His light brown eyes twinkled with mischief as he teased,

“What if he has some heirloom he’s trying to be rid of? Perhaps I should be on hand to ensure he doesn’t dump a big base or a set of drums on us.”

A girl answered when Frances rang the Oldham number asking for Mr. Brentwood and she clearly heard the young voice shouting,

“Dad, a Mrs. Smith for you.”

A man’s deep voice then queried

“Are you the Frances Smith I wrote to?”

“Yes, that’s right. I’m sorry not to have been in touch earlier but I’ve been away and only returned today.”

“I see. My wife Elizabeth is not much interested in Family History and initially I’d like to meet you alone if that’s acceptable to you.”

So it was arranged he should drive over to her the following Wednesday, a day Leonard worked and did not lunch at home.

When Frances answered the doorbell on Wednesday, her eyes travelled upwards to the grey thatch of hair that topped his six feet tall, rugby player frame. With his tanned complexion and cheery smile, he was a surprise. Unlike anything she could have imagined. Their grey eyes and mass of hair seemed to be a common feature between them. Frances must have looked as surprised as she felt, because with a deep chuckle, he said,

"Frances Smith? Were you not expecting me?"

"I'm expecting a Robert Brentwood, but he doesn't look like you." She grinned at him. "Please come inside, coffee's ready. I give you permission to call me Fran as most people do."

Frances heard his exclamation as he followed her into the bright kitchen. Turning, she saw his gaze fixed on a photo hanging in the hall, of Charlie in her degree togs.

"That's Charlie, our youngest child, Charlotte Frances really."

"This is so like our son Robert when he collected his degree, the same features and colouring, the same pose and of course the same gear." He turned to her,

"However, more surprisingly, this girl is also the image of a picture I have of another lady."

He was following her as he talked,

"What is Charlie's degree? Rob did history and archaeology but he's into geology now. Mm! Strange! The likeness to my picture is uncanny."

"Charlie took music and history of music."

Frances chatted about Charlie's musical prowess while she poured coffee and he stood watching her. She felt quite comfortable with him as she chatted. Robert carried a parcel under one arm and he held on to this when seated in the homely comfort of the sitting room with his coffee. Now he placed it on the coffee table and took from it a well wrapped box. Inside this was an old book, which he reverently held in his hands.

"This is the reason I wanted to meet you personally. It's a kind of family heirloom really, that I'm sure you didn't know existed."

Laughter bubbled up inside Frances, spilling out in her voice and he looked at her in quizzical surprise.

"Leonard my husband said you might have a family heirloom to offload and here you are, not daring to let it out of your hands. We have an heirloom too. Look, standing in the corner."

Robert glanced at the cello case and a look of amazement swam across his face as he queried,

"A cello? It can't be. Not THE one belonging to Frances Brown? I had no idea it survived. May I see it?"

Taking the old cello from the modern case, Frances carried the instrument to her guest.

"It was restored a few years ago but the old wood is the same except for an occasional touch of linseed oil to preserve the wood. I have the original bow but we rarely use that; we prefer a modern one. Do you play?"

"I play the piano, mostly jazz." An expression of wonder and reverence creased his features. "Imagine your having this. Incredible. What a beautiful old thing!"

His hands stroked the gleaming wood with surprised wonder then looked up at Fran.

"This must clinch our relationship Fran. We are definitely kin and fairly close kin. Have you drawn up a family tree?"

Frances explained,

"I have only begun looking for my roots this year. For a long time I've wanted to know about her, my Great Gran, but hadn't the sense or time to search and now I have the time, there's nobody alive who can tell me."

From her folder, she found the chart on which was mapped the little she knew and recently discovered. Robert studied this a few moments before clarifying;

"So you have a sister and a brother, your father was Frank who had a sister Charlotte and brother John. They were the children of Hannah Frances, your paternal Grandmother. Did you know she had an older brother Robert Francis, who was my grandfather and the first child of Frances Brown with her first husband Robert Brentwood? Your grandmother Hannah Frances and my grandfather Robert were brother and sister."

Frances' jaw dropped in amazement, "No. I didn't know that. So we are um, half cousins?"

Fondling his book, he nodded and smiled,

"That's correct. I see here on your chart, you have the other son Charles, less than a year younger than Hannah Frances. They were both registered in the name of her second marriage to Elliott."

This was said tongue in cheek but Robert said no more.

Fran looked at him curiously wondering what else was coming.

“Yes I was a while finding her birth. Being so premature she did well to survive in those days. They didn’t have the modern facilities we have today.”

Robert gave her a knowing look and grinned,

“It’s enough to throw anybody off the track.”

Fran poured more coffee as she looked gratefully at her visitor. She felt as though she had known him for years.

“It’s such a thrill for me to find another part of my family and really exciting to learn more of the life of our mutual Gt, Gran. I have an old photo of Gran Hannah Frances with a young man in soldier’s uniform that I think was maybe her brother Charles.”

Fran fished around in the bureau and retrieved a very old photo album to show her visitor.

“Nobody knows anything about him except he was an officer in the army, never married and died in the First World War.”

Frances turned to a postcard size, sepia picture of a dark young soldier standing by a fair haired young woman sitting on a cane chair.

“I think this is Charles with my Gran Hannah Frances.”

Robert studied this before saying,

"I can't verify that as I've not previously seen that photo and have no idea what Charles looked like but you're probably correct."
Fran turned the page to point to another very old sepia photo of a man with bushy dark hair and side whiskers wearing the high collar of the mid 19th century.

"I don't suppose you know who this chap is do you?"
Robert gasped his surprise,

"Well, well. Indeed I do. I have one just like it. That's David, the brother of our Gt. Gran Frances, the first child of her parents, Reverend Robert Brown and Charlotte. If our relationship was not certain before, this proves it."
He picked up his book from the table and held it reverently in his hand to show her.

"Fran, I'm going to leave this journal with you so you can read and enjoy it at your leisure."
He caressed the book lovingly

"You are very honoured. It's never been out of my care since my father entrusted it to me before he enlisted in WW2 with instructions to guard and keep it. My Father was a soldier and died at Dunkirk."
Robert passed the valued volume over the table into Frances' waiting hands.

"Have you ever seen a picture of our Great Grandmother? No? Well, I have a miniature of her with her first husband Robert Brentwood. Now that such excellent copies are available, I'll take some copies and send one to you."

"You have a picture of Frances? I can't believe I will actually see a picture of her. That's more than I ever dreamed. Thank you very much. In return I'll make you a copy of my Hannah Frances who would be your Great Aunt. You know I searched for her birth but couldn't find it because of her early birth."

Robert wagged a finger at her and smiled teasingly,

"Well that's because…"

He broke off mid-sentence then added,

"The book will make everything clear to you."

Robert stayed for a salad lunch and they found they shared many common interests. He remarked there seemed to be one member in each generation who had an affinity with Frances Brown.

"It's remarkable in both our families how we have perpetuated the name, but then she was a remarkable woman in her time, as you will learn when you read her journal."

“Are you telling me this book was actually written by her, by Frances?”

“Oh yes. You didn’t realize? Yes it’s a record of her early years. Not a diary exactly, but almost, more of a confidante really.”

“It’s strange you mention the name threading through the family, it does through ours and like yours, there is one member in each generation who has a close affinity with her and continues her musical skill. My father had it and our daughter Charlie is the only one of our three children.”

Frances told him about the birth of a little girl to their eldest son Thomas and how she was staying there when his letter arrived.

“I wonder if I shall have a grandchild who will be touched by her. Perhaps. I shall have to wait and see if she’s drawn to the cello.”

“I must put another twig on my tree.” Reaching for the cello Robert asked,

“Will you play something for me please?”

Fran prepared the bow and tuned the instrument before settling to play the first part of Elgar’s concerto, then drifted dreamily into the haunting melody that she seemed always to have known. When she finished Robert was silent a few seconds with a strange expression on his face before asking,

“Where did you learn the last piece and what is it called?”

“I don’t know what it is or who wrote it but I’ve always known and loved it.”

Robert looked at her with surprise and picked up his journal. From the back he took a thick piece of manuscript and showed it to Frances.

“That’s what you were playing, it’s titled Nocturne and was written for Frances by her first husband Robert Brentwood, for whom I’m named. You must have seen it somewhere?”

Frances looked a little stunned,

“No I’ve never seen any notation for the music. I can’t remember how I learned it. I think my Gran Hannah played it and my father too.”

Fran passed him a framed photograph of a man in uniform.

“He was a Captain in the navy all through the war and I was just eight when he was killed. I used to sit at his side when he played and vividly remember his last leave, just a few weeks before he died. He played a lot that week and I sat at his feet.”

With misty eyes Frances recalled the last few days she spent with her Father.

“He made a formal will before he left home, because he said he must ensure the cello was safe. My mother hated it and would have pawned it or sent it to the second hand shop."

Robert sighed and commented,

"Yes, the war was a terrible affair and deprived many children of parents."

Frances busied about boiling the kettle and pouring cups of aromatic coffee. Bringing the tray to the table she pressed Robert to help himself to cream as he continued the conversation.

"We will talk some more about all of this Fran, when you know more about our Gt. Gran. If you and your husband are free next Saturday, you could join Elizabeth and me for lunch. There's a pub on the next corner from us that puts on very good lunches. Then you and I can have a couple of hours with the ancestors while our better halves watch telly or have a snooze."

"That sounds a good idea, I'll discuss it with Leonard and let you know on Friday evening, and meanwhile I'll take great care of the precious journal."

CHAPTER SIX

After Robert left, Frances made some more coffee and settled down in her favourite chair to look at the book. It was of dark, tooled leather, about ten inches by eight with "*MY JOURNAL*" written in gold letters on the front. The paper was like parchment, discoloured round the edges and the ink fading. Inside the fly leaf was written in a clear round script the name,

Frances Brown.

Born March 12th. 1847.

This journal was begun by Frances in 1853.

The first pages were written in a round childish hand beginning,

March 18th. 1853. My mother died today with her baby.

May 6th. Father is very unhappy. My brother David is to go away to school soon. A housekeeper is to come and look after us. She will live in the house. Her name is Miss White.

August 10th. The new housekeeper is a very stern lady; she does not like me in the house.

December 25th. It is Christmas day and David is home. I tried to help in the kitchen but Miss White was cross.

February 15th.1854. My little brother George died today; he was five years old and very sick. Miss White would not let me see him until Father said I should. She was cross again.

March 18th. One year since my beloved mother died. Father and I went to put fresh flowers on her grave. Miss White said I should stay here with her but Father said I should go. I go there whenever I can get away, I tell her my troubles.

April 18th. David home for Easter. He is kind to me. I wish I could go away to school. Father teaches me every morning. Miss White says I should be helping her.

August 14th. I have to help Miss White in the mornings now. Father and I have lessons after lunch. The Doctor's daughter Clarice comes for lessons too.

November 2nd. Father is teaching me to play his cello properly now.

January 1st 1855. David returned to college today. He told Father he wishes to be a schoolmaster. It is lonely when he is away.

March 18th. Father has married Miss White. She says I must call her Mother. I will try.

September 24th. I have to hide my journal in Father's study. She is not allowed in there. Clarice still comes for lessons and Father insists I learn also.

April 6th.1856. Father says I play the cello very well but I must learn more lessons. We are reading French now as well as Latin. No books allowed in my room and I am only permitted three hours with Father in the study. The rest of the day is spent cleaning the house, doing laundry and the cooking. Father's income does not stretch to servant help in the house and Mother says why should he when I am here.

July 21st. I have been very ill with scarlet fever. Father nursed me and was very kind but she was afraid she would catch the fever. Father says I am growing too fast and work too hard. He is sending me to stay with his sister in

Morecombe for a whole month. It must be better than here.

August 6th. Father has allowed me to borrow the cello and took me to the coach in the trap. My Uncle Edgar met me with his pony and trap. They live in a lovely warm cottage right by the sea. It is like heaven being here. My Aunt Gertrude is so kind, very like Father, warm and gentle. They have no family but there are always children and people calling in and I am being very spoiled. They will not let me do any work but I am permitted to read and play as much as I like. Uncle Edgar's friend is the schoolmaster and he says I can attend his morning school where he teaches arithmetic, geography and grammar. He will continue to teach me Latin and French after school. The weather is warm and sunny and I have been out to walk with the little dog Meg today.

August 8th. A girl named Ann lives a few cottages along from here and she also attends the school. She and I take Meg for a walk each afternoon after school in the morning. My Aunt Gertrude says I am looking much better and I should be outside all day in the sunshine. Still not allowed to do any work, Aunt says I will have enough when I go home. I dread that day.

August 10th. I am having a wonderful holiday, wrote to tell Father so and tell him thank you for sending me. Aunt asked me about Father's wife today if she was like my mother. I told her the truth. Aunt said if things become too bad, I must leave and come here to stay with them. What heaven but I would miss Father.

August 16th. I am so happy here. Aunt and everybody are really kind and friendly; they laugh a lot about everything. Aunt says if you can laugh even though you are unhappy and feel like crying, things will be easier to bear. Aunt is teaching me embroidery on a cloth.

August 21st. Oh dear, my last week in this heaven. Life could be like this at home if his wife was like Aunt. I do not mind working if she was kind and did not beat me.

August 28th. I have to go home tomorrow. It has been a lovely day, picked berries after lunch, then made pots of jam and jelly. Ann helped and we had such fun. Aunt makes everything fun.

She sat on my bed to talk tonight and says the next time Father's wife strikes me, I must turn on her and threaten to tell Father. Poor Father, he is unhappy enough without my making it worse. Said Goodbye to Ann, I shall miss her but will try to write. I will miss school too. Aunt has written a letter for me to give to Father.

September 14th. Where is heaven? It is worse here, I think Father has said something to his wife; she has not touched me again but treats me badly and allows me no food when Father is away from home.

December 26th. David is here, he returns to college tomorrow. He says I am much too thin but Father's wife has to be kind to me when he or Father is in. David asked me what I am planning to do with my life and says I must give it thought and discuss it with Father.

March 12th. 1857. Today I am eleven. Father's wife says it is time I stopped wasting the afternoons filling my stupid brain with lessons I will never use. She says she will look for a place as scullery maid for me very soon, and then I will know what work is. Father heard and was very angry. Lessons stay.

September 22nd. Today I have a letter from Aunt, Uncle Edgar is bringing her next week and they will stay overnight. The house must be cleaned from top to bottom.

October 1st. Aunt and Uncle have come; it is lovely to see them again. They brought me a letter from Ann. Aunt and Father have long talks together in his study, she is taking me into Oldham tomorrow for new clothes.

October 3rd. Aunt is leaving today; she has told me what to do when my monthly bleeds begin. I have some good warm clothes which fit me and she has turned up the hem of her own thick, blue cloak with the hood and lent it me for the winter. She took a letter I wrote for Ann

April 4th.1858 Father has been ill but his wife would not allow me to see him. Today I crept in and he was very pleased to see me. What would I do without him to protect me?

May 2nd. Father is out and about once more and lessons have recommenced.

December 26th. David is home. He has begun university in

Oxford. I should so love to be able to go with him.

March 11th. 1859 My monthly bleeds have begun. Bless Aunt; I am so grateful to her.

July 5th. Aunt has died with the influenza. Father is very upset; I understand she was his only family. Said he and I would attend the funeral but his wife wishes to go. Have written to Uncle Edgar. What will I do without Aunt, she was so kind to me and I loved her.

November 17th. Squire Porter asked Father if I would like to help his wife with their small children when she has her new baby next Easter. Father says he will think about it. Would I like to go on condition I am not a skivvy? What would be the difference between that and what

I am here? They have lots of servants at the hall.

February 16th.1861 Father very ill, asking to see me. He has made a will and left it at his bank. He has left me all his books and his cello. Asked his wife to send for Doctor Turner but I do not think she did so. Father told me he will not get better. I am desolate. What will I do if he leaves me with her?

February 19th. Father died on Wednesday 17th. The funeral was today. His wife told me to pack my things in a little trunk. She has found me a position as kitchen maid. Squire Porter spoke to me at the funeral and said the post of governess and nanny to his children is there if I want it. I said yes thank you.

February 20th. Father's bank manager came to the Vicarage after the funeral and told his widow about the will. He said he would have all the books and everything from Father's study, crated up and stored for me. The cello I am to keep with me. Father's widow was furious as she knew nothing about the will. I am packed and ready to leave this house and shall never return whilst she is here. The only reason I have stayed this long was for Father. At least I have David or I would be alone in the world. Father's wife thinks I am going to that old skinflint at the Manor when I shall be going in the other direction to the Hall. No doubt she will soon find her mistake. She will have to leave the Vicarage soon.

<u>February 25th. 1861</u> I am becoming settled. Have my own room in the nursery suite, next to old Nanny Simpson. She was Nanny to Mrs Porter. The Squire and Mrs Porter are very kind to me. I know exactly what my duties are. Wash and dress Nicholas four and Judith two and breakfast with them. Then we do activities and easy lessons until eleven o-clock, before a walk, whatever the weather. Lunch at twelve thirty then the children spend an hour with their parents before taking a rest. While they are resting, I have mending or sewing to do. When they rise we do more activities then a walk and play outside before nursery tea. We have some games, then a bath, after which the parents visit the nursery for an hour before story time and bed at

seven o-clock. Nanny is a kind, bustly person. Sometimes I teach the children little songs and am allowed to play my beloved cello after the children have retired.

March 11th. Hard to believe I will be fourteen tomorrow. Took the children and some fresh flowers to the churchyard for Father's grave this morning. It is looking very neglected. I will bring a tool and tidy it tomorrow. I miss Father so much. I can only learn what I can teach myself now. Squire Porter has given me use of the library; he is a kind man and was fond of Father.

March 28th. The new baby boy has arrived and keeps Nanny very busy. He sleeps in his Mother's room.

April 7th. The flowers I put on Father's grave were tipped out and the vase smashed. Fresh flowers in a pot there instead. Found a metal vase and replaced my flowers at his feet. The children love their walks, we saw blackthorn blossom today and found a blackbird's nest with two eggs.

<u>July 4th</u>. Squire Porter's younger brother is home from university. Very handsome and charming but frightens me. He does not like the children and keeps interrupting our activities.

<u>September 2nd</u>. The Squire's brother has gone thank heaven. He was a nuisance and kept trying to kiss me and get me into a corner. The Squire caught him one morning and was very angry. Letter from David, he has a position as a junior teacher in a big school in Oldham.

November 1st. Frosty this morning and very cold. Collected some fir cones to dry for Christmas decorations. Found a young owl with an injured leg. Took him to the groom, Mr. Coles. He let the children watch as he strapped up its leg. He keeps him in a cage in the stables until the leg mends. Mr Coles says the children can feed young owl each day and named him Hoppy.

December 24th. Christmas Eve, I have never known such a day. The children helped me to dress the tree and we brought out all the decorations they have been drying and painting for weeks. Squire's brother home again but is behaving himself.

Dec.26th. There is to be a ball tonight in the ballroom. The great hall looks splendid with the decorations. The mistress has given me permission to watch from the gallery. She seems very pleased with me and I like it here. I love the children, they are so good.

Dec.28th. I have run away. Master Nicholas forced himself upon me and threw me onto the floor and himself on top of me. I do not know what would have happened had the squire not come into the library. He must have suspected something. Master Nicholas caught me first in the gallery and tried to get me down, but I bit him and managed to escape. Then I hid in the library where he never goes, but he found me. I cannot stay here longer. The squire will find my note, I hate leaving the children but I must go. I have a little money saved and must find another position. I am walking to Oldham.

Jan. 3rd. 1862. The journey was long and I walked all the way except a few miles on a carrier's cart. I was exhausted when I arrived here. I brought the cello with me, slung across my back. This made my journey even harder. David was very surprised to see me. He has a room in his headmaster's cottage where there is a wife and four children. They have found me a temporary room at the vicarage. In return for teaching the youngest schoolchildren I will have board and lodge. They cannot pay me but it will give me time to look for a position. I miss my children and I think they will be missing me. I will send for my things when I am settled.

Jan.20th. the children here are poor, rough little things, but pleasant and willing. I have to teach them numbers and letters, songs and poetry; also I take them for nature walks and read them stories. The Head teacher bothers me. He is a large, forceful man, loud in his manner. He always seems to be behind me or watching me and has the same look in his eyes as the Squire's brother. I must find a new position quickly.

Feb.4th. David has a friend whose uncle is a church school teacher near Manchester. There is a position there for a teacher of the infant class. I am going there to begin on Monday. The Headmaster here is angry but David has noticed how he pesters me all the time.

Feb.9th. Travelled here by carrier's cart, only six miles from Manchester which is a big, dirty town. This is a church school and Mr. Summers, the schoolteacher, is quite an old man whose wife is semi-invalid. There is a room here and board, but my pay will be only one shilling a month, because of my lack of qualifications and experience. At least it will give me some breathing space to look for something better. David is looking for a Headmaster post; he wants to get away from his current principal.

March 12th. My fifteenth birthday. Poor Mr. Summers works very hard; I do not know how he managed alone. I wash his wife and help to sit her up in a chair, before we have breakfast, usually porridge I set on the night before. Poor lady had a seizure last year but can speak a little.

We are in school for eight forty five and lessons begin at nine am. Mr. Summers is a kind, fair man but very strict with the children. My infant class numbers twenty under seven years and his top class twenty nine. I try to make lessons a game and I am making some impression, they are progressing. The children go home or bring a sandwich. It is usually bacon and egg for us at lunch-time because it is quick and easy. Then we attend Mrs. Summer's toilette and if there are a few minutes to spare, I have begun speech lessons with her.

We found violets on our walk this afternoon and the hawthorn hedgerows are showing green pips.

The children have not been taken out for nature walks before and they love it. We took the violets to Mrs. Summers, she enjoyed seeing the children and it is good for them to see a sick person. The little ones leave early so I have time to do some hand exercises with Mrs. Summers and we are practicing a few steps. We want to surprise Mr. Summers. Then I make a stew or pie for supper. Mrs. Summers sits to table now and tries very hard to use her poor hand.

July 30th. The children left school for their harvest holiday this afternoon; we shall see them no more until September when all is gathered in. The inspector has been in school this week to test the children and says I am not qualified to teach and he will find a proper teacher as soon as he can. Mr. Summers was very upset, he says Mrs. Summers is making such good progress and is a different person since I came. He says the children have made wonderful headway too, much better than if he had the whole school himself. Out of my twenty, twelve can read well, five moderately and even the three youngest can read a few words and know the alphabet.

August 12th. During the school break Mr. Summers and I have whitewashed the walls inside the classrooms, painted all the windows and cleaned everything. It all looks very clean and smart now, ready for the children returning. I made a new alphabet on the clean walls with coloured chalks. It has all the letters, capital and lower case and pictures of things the children will know. It looks very grand, Mr. Summers brought his wife to see, and they were both pleased with it.

September 1st. No new teacher has appeared so Mr. Summers asked me to stay on. I am happy to do that because they are such good people and I love the children. Mrs. Summers is so much better now, we walked to the door to meet Mr. Summers and he was surprised and delighted. Her being able to walk will make his life much easier. I wish I could find a more permanent position.

December 23rd. The children have been making lovely Christmas decorations and pictures and I have taught them a nativity play. We are to perform it tomorrow for all the school, the Vicar and Mrs. Summers.

December 25th. Christmas day. The play was a great success; the children were wonderful and sang the carols we learned to the cello. We were given a large cockerel and Mrs. Summers helped me to cook the lunch. It was such a bright, sunny day, after lunch I took a long walk then came back to a big log fire Mr. Summers made.

February 10th.1863. Mr. and Mrs. Summers have died in the influenza epidemic. They were both buried today. My friends have gone, I have lost them. The inspector is sending a new schoolmaster and he needs the cottage. Mr. Summers has left me everything and £20.00 as well as my wages. The things from the house are going to David's cottage, he can use them until I am settled and he says I can stay with him until then.

March $12^{th.}$ My sixteenth birthday. I am still with David in his cottage, a bit like home with the Summers' belongings. I have written to the Squire asking him to send my things and to Father's bank manager to dispatch the books etc. David will be well set up then. He likes his new position in the church school of Amberley. There are fifty pupils and he has an infant teacher who lives a few doors down from the school. I am going to try and play with the Manchester City New Orchestra. Tomorrow I shall go and see the conductor.

March 14th. Mr. Brentwood is a charming man, he heard me play and commended me, but said he could not take me into the orchestra. He was very nice but said he had forty male players and could not take the risk of my being the only female and exposed to that danger. If only I were a man!

May 4th. I have been helping to teach the infants in David's school because their teacher is ill. Met David's lady friend today. Clarissa is a housemaid in a large house belonging to one of the mill owners.

July 30th. School breaks today. Discussed my plan with David. He is against it but says he will help all he can if I am determined. A new teacher has been appointed to begin in September and Clarissa wants to *be married. I must find work, my savings are dwindling.*

CHAPTER SEVEN

The telephone shrilled and Frances was catapulted unwillingly back to the present and her own sitting room. Amy's voice squeaked,

"Has your visitor been? What was he like? Why did he come and what did he have to show you?

"Hold on there, one thing at a time." Fran stopped her with a laugh.

"Yes he's been and he's a big, cheerful chap. He came to show me a book I've begun to read. It's very enlightening. And, what do you think Amy? He has a picture of my great Grandmother with her first husband and is going to make a copy for me. He's invited Len and me over to their house this coming Saturday. I just cannot believe this is really happening."

"That's just wonderful. I wish something like that would turn up in my family. Are you shopping tomorrow, if so I'll meet you in town and you can fill me in."

After replacing the phone, Frances thought ruefully that it was too late to continue the journal. Leonard would want tea early so that he could attend the Neighbourhood Watch meeting this evening. Well she could read more while alone later, with her feet up the chimney. The telephone rang again while she was preparing the meal. This time it was Peter.

"Good afternoon Mum, are you in this evening?"

"Hello there Peter and how are you?"

"I'm fine and I'll call in on the way to Oldham. Have a meeting there and I'll have a young lady with me. Is there any chance of a nosh with you? Just salad or something quick."

"Of course dear I'll fix you something. Is this young lady somebody we've met before or a new model?"

"New model Ma. She's a stunner. See you around fivish. Bye now."

Peter was a computer programmer with a high tech. company in Manchester and was always whizzing around the country with glamorous girls trailing after him or hanging on to his terminals. That was her dream of peace shattered.

Amy met up with Fran in their favourite coffee shop in town the next morning and they settled in to a quiet corner to enjoy a natter.

Fran began the conversation by telling her friend about Peter calling with yet another female companion the previous evening.

"So what's this one like? He's brought a few to see you hasn't he."

"I've lost count, but this one is a model, thin and fragile. I cooked some salmon and served a salad and crusty bread but she hardly ate anything. Otherwise she was very pleasant. Don't think she'll last long. Peter will lose patience with her faddiness 'cos he has a good appetite."

Amy hung her jacket round the back of her chair and put her packages on the spare chair with Fran's bags.

"Your Peter certainly pulls in the dames. Now come on out with the real news, I can't wait to hear about this new man in your life." Amy's face was alight with eagerness, brown eyes sparkling.

"Steady on there. Hang on a minute."

The waitress served their coffee and scones and Fran waited until she'd left them alone.

"A knock at the door and there stood this big guy, grey curly hair, a bit like a larger masculine version of me, very cheery and friendly. As he came into the house he noticed Charlie's photo in the hall and exclaimed in surprise. He said it was similar to one they have of their son Rob. But this bit is interesting Amy, also very like a picture he has of another young woman."

Amy excited voice chimed in,

"Who's that picture of Fran? Hurry up and get to the point."

With a huge smile on her face Fran calmly buttered her scone and sliced it in half before replying,

"First of all he followed me into the kitchen with this parcel under his arm and waited while I made the coffee and carried it through to the sitting room. I pulled his leg about Len wondering if he was trying to offload an ancient artifact and him there clutching this package to his breast."

Fran could see Amy squirming with impatience and sipped her coffee before continuing,

"He put down his package and out of a box he lifted this quite big book and laid it on the table. He said the book belonged to Frances my Gt. Grandmother and he guarded it with his life."

Amy gulped in amazement saying,

"Wow. You didn't expect that. That is awesome! Go on."

"I told him we owned a relic too and it was behind him in the corner. I took it out and showed him the cello and like you, he couldn't believe his eyes. He was just overwhelmed."

They finished their coffee as Fran told Amy,

"He identified that photo I have of the man with whiskers as the brother of Frances and he comes into the story of her life."

After Fran had updated Amy with all her news and they finished their elevenses, Fran picked up her parcels ready to leave and said,

"As Rob left he told me that Frances had written the journal about her experiences and I could keep it to read. He invited Len and me to go over there to return it."

Pushing back their chairs they turned to leave as Amy said,

"You know I'm green with envy about your luck but so pleased for you, because you wanted to know her story and it looks like you are to learn about her life. Did you say you've started to read it?"

They left the shop still chatting and walked to where Amy's car was parked near Fran's locked bicycle.

"Yes I've started but there is a lot of it and don't think I'll finish before the weekend. I'll pop in at yours later in the week to show you Amy. See you then."

It was the following afternoon before Frances contrived an opportunity for a few hours uninterrupted solitude. The shopping put away and lunch cleared, Len had gone to a meeting and rain slashed against the windows. Frances buried herself in the big arm-chair with a cup of tea at her elbow and a log fire crackling up the chimney.

CHAPTER EIGHT

September 1st. David has found me lodgings in Manchester, Mrs. Askew is a kind, motherly soul, used to be cook at Squire Porter's until her marriage and remembers Father. She wears her dark hair back in a bun and is a plump rosy lady. Have confided my plan to her, she thinks it a huge joke. She has given me a pair of spectacles with plain glass which will be a big help.

September 3rd. Today I became a member of the Manchester City Orchestra and changed my name to Mr. Francis Brown. I was terrified Mr. Brentwood would recognize me or the way I play. Despite my fear of being found out and my nervousness, when he heard me play he took me on trial for one month. My plan to disguise myself as a man has worked so far. David's clothes fit well since I altered them and Mrs. Askew cut my hair and dressed it as some men wear theirs, tied back with a black velvet bow. If only I were not so small and skinny. I think wearing the spectacles, makes me look quite manly. If I do not speak to anybody it could work. Mrs. Askew laughed until she cried. Neither of us thought it could work but the adventure is just beginning. I will need to be very careful all of the time.

<u>October 3rd.1864</u>. The orchestra practice each morning and gives concerts at least weekly. It seems very popular, usually sold out.

Mr. Brentwood said today,

“Your trial period was satisfactory Mr. Brown and I am happy to offer you a contract. Ahem.”

He paused and looked very uncomfortable,

“Because you are so young, I feel I should warn you that you must be wary of some members of the orchestra. I would like to think you feel able to tell me if there are problems.”

I wasn’t sure what he was warning me of and he seemed very embarrassed.

Some of the men treat me with scorn or indifference and ignore me. Some are very strange and over friendly but most are helpful. It is very different playing with an orchestra to playing alone. A few very anxious moments on technicalities.

Mr. Brentwood is a wonderful man. He gives concerts with cheap and even free seats so that poor people may listen. Sometimes in the summer, he gives open-air concerts in the park, which means anyone can listen. He believes all should have the benefit of music.

December 12th. There is a busy program from now until after Christmas and Messrs. Crossley, double base and Dixon, violin, are making themselves troublesome. They keep inviting me to visit their lodgings and Mr. Crossley touches me at every opportunity. They both sit in my section and Mr. Brentwood is very observant and pointedly takes an interest in my playing, I think to protect me. I am not afraid of him but am frightened by the others. When will I ever be safe? Is there something wrong with me that attracts undesirable men?

December 15th. Mr. Brentwood stopped me today and asked,

"Mr Brown, may I ask where you are lodging and with whom."

"Yes Sir, I will write it down for you but request please, that you do not disclose it to others."

He looked at me strangely and said,

"I quite understand Mr Brown."

Mrs Askew found me some clothes her son has outgrown which are dark and make me look older. (More masculine?) I will soon have saved enough money to buy a new coat but how will I obtain it? Mrs. Askew says her sister could make trousers but would not attempt a coat. Perhaps a ladies outfitter will make me one or maybe Mr. Askew could help, am sure he would if I ask him. Mr. Askew runs a carriage business and his wife cleans them and tends the horses. I could not have better lodgings than with this kindly couple. He is rough and ready, large and florid, but such a gentle man. They are very kind to me and interested in all I do.

David is marrying Clarissa on December 24th. and I can attend the wedding. There was a slight unpleasantness with Mr. Crossley today. I was careless and he pressed me against the wall and tried to kiss me. Horrible man, he must suspect I am female. Mr.Brentwood interrupted and said

"Mr. Crossley, stop that at once. Mr. Brown is here to practice and work, he is not a toy for you to play with."

Strange words! Mr. Dixon calls me names like 'Mr. Brentwood's darling' and 'sweetheart'. I must be more careful. I think Mr. Dixon was trying to follow me today but I knew he was there and took a side road. I asked Mrs Aiskew about these weird men. She didn't look surprised at their behaviour but told me.

"There are certain unusual men who fall in love with young boys instead of girls. Be very careful and keep out of their way."

<u>December 30th.1864</u> David and Clarissa were married at noon on Christmas Eve, it was a sunny day and all went well. I hope they will be happy. It seemed so strange to be wearing a gown again after trousers and jacket.

David says there will always be a home there if I should need one; I am not so sure Clarissa would be happy about that.

Been very busy with extra concerts and recitals, which required extra rehearsals. Mr. Brentwood came to my lodgings on Christmas Day and asked if he could speak to me. Mrs. Askew consulted me first and I had to do a quick change into my usual male apparel. I said I would see him if the Askews were present and he agreed. He said he wished to make sure my lodgings were good and that I was safe.

"Mr. Brown, you are very young and perhaps I should not have allowed you into the orchestra, but you have a rare talent that we can use."

Again he looked very uncomfortable as he looked down at me sitting on the couch.

"You are also very unworldly and I suspect, have not met men such as Messer Crossley and Dixon before. There are other players who prefer young men to young female company, but those two are the most flagrant."

He stopped as Mrs. Askew put her arm around my shoulders. I sensed my face and neck becoming red and hot and felt quite sick. He continued after a while.

"Although I can protect you in working time, I have no power to stop them following you here and pestering you."

"Thank you for your protection and care of me Sir, I am most grateful and will be very vigilant. However, I do have to walk back and forth and cannot always escape their notice."

"May I suggest Mr. Brown, that instead of carrying your cello back here to your lodgings each day, you leave it in my room. This will make it much easier for you to travel and go down alleys, should you need to escape. I can easily transport the instrument in my carriage, to rehearsals or wherever."

"Thank you Sir that will be a great help and enable me to run if needs be."

"If I may be so personal Mr. Brown, may I suggest also that you grow some side whiskers and maybe a moustache? It is your very youth that attracts them to you."

I thought Mrs. Askew would explode and could feel her quivering beside me. What a kind man he is to be so concerned. When he had gone I asked Mrs. Askew,

"Do you think he is one of those people who prefer young men?"

She laughed, holding her sides and the tears running off her chin and said,

"Bless you love, no, but you might have to watch out when he finds you're a lass. The thought of you growing whiskers and moustaches. Oh deary, deary me. That's rich, that is."

I do feel bad about deceiving him but it has to be. What can I do against these men? Mr. Askew says he will give me some lessons in self-defence and will find me a small cosh which will fit my inside coat pocket.

March 12th 1865.

My seventeenth birthday. I feel much older but do not look any older. My life would be so much easier if my face did not look so girlish and my complexion so fair. Last night Mr. Askew met me after the concert because the previous evening, Mr. Crossley came behind me on the way home and pushed me into a yard. He is a big, heavy man and was trying to unfasten my trousers but I managed to get out the cosh while he was slobbering all over me. I hit him hard on the head. He was so stunned that I hit him a few more times and blew hard on my whistle, then ran all the way home. Both the Askews are worried that they will join forces to attack me. What am I to do?

Mr. Crossley had a large bruise on his cheek today and glared at me fiercely. Must have more lessons in self-defence.

July 27th. More unpleasantness, this time with Mr. Dixon. He caught me leaving my cello in Mr. Brentwood's office and put his arms around me to kiss me and press himself against me. He says he loves me and begs me to go back to his lodgings just around the corner adding,

"Why should Brentwood have all the good things?"

I managed to break free by striking him with my knee just as Mr.Brentwood came to his office. I ran but I could hear Mr. Brentwood calling after me. I cannot understand why grown men love boys.

August 8th. Mr. Brentwood came to see me at my lodgings this afternoon. He looked very serious when he told me,

"I have given a final warning to both Mr. Dixon and Mr. Crossley. I am aware of the incident with the latter and am very worried about your safety."

Mr. Brentwood paused and looked over my head,

"I wonder Mr. Brown if you would consider lodging at my house as my protégé. My sister lives with me and I have a housekeeper and a butler and everything would be in order. I think I could give you my full protection if I convey you back and forth."

His eyes rested at last upon me and his gaze softened,

"I feel it is no longer safe for you to be out alone child, especially when dark and late."
I was stunned and replied,

"I thank you kindly Sir but I am happy here with Mr and Mrs Askew. However, I will think over your offer."

How could I stay with him, he would find me out within a day and his sister would see through me even sooner. I have seen her at times at the concerts with a dubious looking man.

<u>September 6th.</u> Mr. Brentwood called me as I was leaving rehearsal this morning.

"Mr. Brown, have you thought over my suggestion of yesterday?"

"Yes Sir, I have given much thought to what you said and discussed it with the Askews. I am most grateful for your concern about my welfare, but have decided to stay where I am for the moment."

I thought it may cause problems for him; it certainly would for me if I were under his roof!

"I think Mr. Brown, if you have any more problems, the only way to protect you, will be to let you go."

"Oh no Mr. Brentwood, I do so love playing with you, I mean with the orchestra and I would have the same problems wherever I was."

"Yes that may be true, but I feel responsible for you while you are still so young and I do not want any harm to befall you."

Oh dear. I am becoming very attached to this man; he is so kind and caring. As though my *life has not sufficient complications.*

CHAPTER NINE

Peace was shattered as the outer door opened to admit Leonard, home earlier than usual.

"It's still pouring with rain and very chilly out there. I suddenly thought you would have a good fire going and it would be more comfortable at home." He grinned at me as he came to the fire rubbing his hands to warm them.

Frances abandoned the journal until a more favourable time; she felt she must be alone to read this very private record. They were having tea when Charlie rang to ask if she could borrow the car on Saturday.

"I have a concert in Manchester City Hall and mine requires attention before going for M.O.T. next Monday."

Leonard explained,

"We will need the car love, but as we are going in the same direction, I'm sure we can work something out Charlie, it's an opportunity for you to meet your Mother's newly found relatives. We're having lunch with them and they live between here and Manchester."

"Thanks Dad, I just couldn't face lugging a cello on public transport. See you on Friday night."

There was a Family History meeting the next evening and Amy was full of question when they met. Frances brought her up to date but explained that as she'd promised to return the journal on Saturday, there wouldn't be time for Amy to have more than a passing glance.

The speaker was very knowledgeable about dating photographs and portraits by the way they were mounted, the dress of the subject and the style of the pose. She displayed slides of costumes to illustrate the various periods and showed good examples of early lithographs, through to the beautiful sepia pictures of the nineteenth and early twentieth century. Frances thought the picture Robert promised would either be an early photograph from the mid eighteen hundreds or a portrait and was looking forward to seeing it with excited impatience.

The following morning, Frances found the post brought the usual bills, a brief note from Thomas with a snapshot of Janet and a very content looking Bethany. Thomas thanked her again for her stay and for easing Janet through the early days which are so fraught with anxiety and worry. Janet appeared quite relaxed and was enjoying caring for a baby who was so happy, if only she wasn't permanently hungry. They were managing to have four or five hours sleep at night, which was more than he ever achieved as a houseman in hospital.

The missive she purposely left until last was a cardboard cylinder with an Oldham postmark. Now with trembling fingers, she carefully snipped off the sellotape sealing the end. Gently withdrawing the contents a thin rolled card, revealed a studio sepia photograph of a man standing with a much younger woman seated beside and in front of him. A formal picture, the man was dressed in a fine coat and breeches, shirt with lace showing at the cuff and a ruffled lace cravat. He looked a tall handsome man with the side-whiskers of the time and a small dark moustache. The young woman wore a dress of lighter fabric adorned with lace at throat and cuffs. It was the face of the girl that caused Frances to sit down quickly with shock. The features were dainty, well arched brows over large eyes, the nose delicate and pointed, the mouth soft and well-shaped, the chin pointed and delicate. Her colouring appeared fair on the picture much lighter than the man. A small dimple was apparent at the side of the smiling lips. It was like looking at a picture of Charlie. No wonder Robert had been taken with that photo, he said it was like his Rob but also like another picture. She shivered as a thought forced itself into her mind. Frances wished she could remember the family tree Robert showed her; tomorrow she would ask to see it again. Were they more closely related than she thought?

When Fran used a magnifying glass on the photo she could clearly see the ring finger of the woman's left hand showed two rings...

The day was pleasant and warm and Leonard was busy mowing the lawns. Normally Frances would have spent the afternoon pottering around the flower beds but instead she disappeared into the summerhouse with the journal.

CHAPTER TEN

January 4th. 1865

The Christmas period has been full of special concerts and recitals in private houses and halls. The two demons have been quiet, does that mean they have given up or are they plotting their next move. I play a constant game of cat and mouse trying to evade them and keeping one step ahead. They are very aware Mr. Brentwood has given me his protection and call me his 'little concubine'.

I have played one or two solo pieces and wonder if this may be the way to go for me.

February 1ST. Last night I was kidnapped by the two devils who were one either side of me and had a carriage waiting. They just picked me up and lifted me inside but not before I screamed. Mr. Crossley said

"You have been invited to my rooms so many times and have refused; now we are taking you and there is no Mr Brentwood to help you this time. He has had his fun, now it is our turn. He has to learn to share his toys."

Mr. Dixon took my hand and was making me touch his knees and legs and Mr. Crossley was kissing my face and neck with his wet mouth. I was terrified and wriggled to the floor and curled into a ball while trying to get out my whistle.

"You little beauty, we have waited a long time for you. I can teach you how real men love little boys."

The carriage stopped and they bundled me out, but I bent

over and put the whistle in my mouth and blew and blew until they snatched it away. By then I had my cosh loose and set about their heads. I knew I could not win them both but I could make a fuss. Then a familiar coach stopped and down jumped Mr. Askew. Another carriage drew in and it was all over. I was much bruised and shaken but the two demons were in worse shape. Mr. Brentwood. (It was he in the second carriage) picked me up while Mr. Askew was laying into the demons. I was so relieved and grateful to my saviours that I leaned against Mr. Brentwood's chest and wept. I could feel his surprise but he put his arms around me and said,

"There my child, you are quite safe now. I do not think they will bother you again. See here is a man of the law; it is to prison with them."

Mr. Askew came up then saying,

"All right sweeting, let us have you home now. Yes Mr. B, perhaps you should come too."

I felt sufficiently recovered to look up into Mr. Brentwood's face and could see his puzzlement.

When we were in the house, Mrs. Askew was told the happenings and fussed over me. When she went away to make some tea taking Mr. Askew with her, Mr. Brentwood stood looking down at me with his hands on my shoulders.

"Now Mr. Brown, you have some explaining to do I think?"

He did not sound angry, but had every right to be. I could not look at him.

"I am sorry Sir to have deceived you, but I needed work desperately and could not play as a woman. I wanted so badly to be with your orchestra."

There was a silence and I could feel him watching me and sense him shaking. When at last I dared to look up at him, he was convulsed with laughter.

"I should put you over my knee and spank you, little minx. To think I have been trying to protect you all this time from those animals and if they had known what I now know, they would not have been interested."

"What will happen? Do I have to leave you?"

"What do you think I should do? Do you wish to leave?" He asked looking at me sternly.

"No. Oh please no. I could not bear it if you sent me away I love playing with you---your orchestra."

My hands clasped together I entreated him, my last words a whisper.

"Mm, mm. There is one way you could stay but it may not be acceptable to you."

"Anything Sir, if I can only stay. What is your proposal?"

Putting his hands again on my shoulders he waited until I looked at him,

"It really is a proposal. You could marry me. That way you could still play and I would not lose an excellent cellist, yet could give you my full protection at all times."

Mad thoughts of him loving me swept through my mind and

joy flooded my face as I stammered,

"M-marry you? But-"

My sentence trailed off in confusion.

"I have become very fond of you and have no wish to lose you," then added quickly

"it need be in name only."

The gladness died inside me. Well how dare I dream a great man like this could possibly love me. After all, he thought I was a boy until half an hour ago.

"If my suggestion is not distasteful to you, will you do something for me er, Mr. Brown?"

"Yes Sir I will do anything I can for you."

"Mm. Will you go and change into a gown please, so that I can formally propose to you?"

In less than ten minutes, I was divested of my male attire and dressed in my one good gown. As I quickly redressed my hair, my mind was busily turning over this latest development. I was more than surprised; I was amazed and a little frightened. If he just wanted a marriage in name only, how would I manage that? My future was assured and I would be safe, but how could I hide my real feelings for him. I knew I loved this man, honoured and respected him above everybody. I needed time.

When I returned to the parlour, Mr. Askew whistled and I heard Mr. Brentwood draw in his breath sharply as he rose to his feet. Mrs. Askew presented me with a flourish,

"Miss Frances Brown."

Mr. Brentwood took my hand and kissed it and there was warm gentleness in his voice,

"My pleasure my dear Miss Brown. We have met before I think?"

Hot blood flooded my face

"You remember?"

"Yes indeed. I cannot think why I failed to recognize you before. There has always been something familiar in the way you play and now I know why. I was very impressed with your performance the day you called to see me the first time. Perhaps the spectacles have put me off."

I felt my face hot again as, keeping my hand in his he said

"Miss Brown, before witnesses I again request this hand in marriage."

The Askews exclaimed in surprise and I stammered,

"But you know nothing about me. What will your sister think?"

"I know that you have beauty, spirit and courage and that you play the cello divinely. What more do I need to know? My sister will be delighted that I am to marry at last. She has tried to find me a wife many times but I never met anybody I wanted to spend my life with."

My hands were very comfortable nestled in his much larger ones.

"You do not need to give me your answer until you have taken time to think it over. Write to your brother, take some time off to visit him and discuss it before you decide. I will ask you again in two weeks."

“Thank you, yes I should like to do that. I appreciate the great honour you have shown me and thank you for it.”

February 10TH.1865. I visited David and Clarissa to discuss my situation. David has given his approval of the marriage if that is what I wish. Clarissa was pleased I am not wanting a home with them and did not like it when David reminded me to take any of Father’s things I wanted. I shall take one or two books, the rest belongs as much to David as to me.

February 12th1865 Mr Brentwood proposed to me again today saying

“My dear Frances, I know I have not waited the two weeks I told you but I am impatient for your answer. Will you marry me?”

I answered him gladly,

"I accept your proposal and will try to be a good wife and make you happy."

Mr. Brentwood and I are to be married almost immediately; he has announced our engagement to the members of the orchestra. They were highly amused after their initial shock.

March 10th. 1864. The wedding at eleven this morning went very well. David and Clarissa stood for me and Mr. Brentwood's sister Eleanor and his friend and solicitor William Elliott were also witnesses. The service was in the Parish Church and we came back here for the wedding breakfast. Daily rehearsal was postponed and continues as usual tomorrow morning. There is a concert in the Town Hall in the evening. I have been performing in female dress and expect there will be the usual hum of remarks and prattle at there being a woman in the orchestra. I am an attraction and feel it is a peep show. Perhaps Mr. Brentwood will take in more women now; he says they are equally as good players as men.

So today I became Mrs. Brentwood and tonight I should have been bedded and made a wife but it seems he really does want a marriage in name only. After we dined and returned to our parlour, we played a game of chess. I have not played since living with David. I was very on edge not knowing what to expect. Then he escorted me to the door of this room and said,

"This is your very own room child and nobody will ever disturb you here unless by your invitation. I hope you have everything you need, if there is anything at all you want, just tell me or your maid Patty. Sleep well my very dear Frances; I will see you at eight-o-clock for breakfast."

With a hand each side my face, he kissed my forehead. Oh, how I wanted to put my arms around him for more kisses. I must be content. I did not think my wedding night would be like this.

CHAPTER ELEVEN

The sound of the lawn mower spluttered and ceased near the summerhouse and Leonard announced his intention of putting on the kettle for a cup of tea. My concentration broken, I let my mind wander over the exploits of this remarkable woman. I realized I would need to sit up half the night to finish the tale. Leonard returned with the tea and sat beside me for a well-earned rest. Picking up the journal he mused,

"This must be very interesting to stop you picking up a trowel this pleasant afternoon."

"Yes Leonard, it's powerful cloak and dagger stuff. I'll have to return it unfinished and beg Mr. Brentwood to loan it to me a while longer. That means another trip over there, I couldn't risk sending it through the post, it's far too valuable."

Holding the book in front of him he chortled,

"Valuable, this old relic? You mean like 'The Diary of an Edwardian lady?'"

"Well yes, something like that. It's more the confidante of a lonely, young woman trying to make her way in a man's world. A factual record of her life one hundred and fifty years ago."

There was no further opportunity to dip into the journal that day. Charlie unloaded herself and her belongings at teatime that evening. Cellos, piles of music, coats and bags overflowed from the hall into the kitchen. I was struck again by the likeness between the picture and this daughter of ours. Impulsive, vigorous and talented, Charlie moved through the world like a fresh spring breeze from the mountains, until she sat down to play. Then, the magic flowed from beneath her fingers and wrapped itself around you like a melodic mantle. The thought burst through my head again and impatience seized me. A longing to know more of what only the journal could tell me.

When she went into the sitting room, Charlie immediately saw the new picture on the mantel and her surprised voice called,

"Mum. Who's this new photo of? Where did you find it?"

"Well who do you think it could be?"

"Looks like it could be family. I bet that new chap sent it. Is it his mother?"

"Not a bad try. It's his Gt Grandmother and may be mine too."

"Heavens I didn't realize you were that far into your family. What's his name?"

"His name is Robert and his son is Rob. The family is peppered with Roberts. You will meet some of them tomorrow."

After Charlie had retired Leonard took his book to bed and I took the journal and was soon whizzed back to the 19th. Century and what happened next.

CHAPTER TWELVE

April

Robert arranged for us to visit a studio to have something called a photograph picture taken after our wedding.

Trying to fit into this strange household is difficult. Miss Eleanor is a tall well-dressed woman with very dark hair worn up and curled at the sides. She wears paint and powder on her face which makes her look very artificial. She treats me very civilly but I have the strong feeling she thinks her brother married beneath him, as indeed he has. Wicks is a dear old footman come butler, Mrs Hopwood the cook and Patty the parlourmaid who also helps me. There is also an outside man.

Mr. Elliott is a cold fellow whose smile does not reach his icy grey eyes. He is short and thick set with black hair and side whiskers. I find him repulsive and quite fearsome. He often visits to discuss business with Robert.

July 2nd. Mr. Brentwood, he says I must call him Robert, has written a solo cello piece and dedicated it to me. It is the most beautiful and haunting melody. I played it as a solo for the first time tonight and the audience loved it. He is the gentlest of men and I am hurt and upset because he will not take me as his wife. He gives me every indication both in public and in private life, that he loves me and I show him all the time that I love him deeply. What more can I do?

August 30th. Yesterday evening Robert knocked at my door as I was dressing my hair. He entered at my invitation and stood behind me, watching me in the mirrors. He said,

"I have a present for you and wondered if you would like to wear it for this special performance tonight."

He opened a velvet case and took out the most magnificent necklet of emeralds, not huge nor heavy but dainty and exquisite. He fastened it around my throat while I held up my hair, which has grown long again. He kissed the back of my neck then said in a strange muffled voice,

"You are a very beautiful girl Frances. Are you happy here with me?"

His question took me by surprise and I felt the tears sting my eyes and spill over. I could not speak. He continued,

"Frances, my dearest, is something wrong? What is it? What can I do?"

The tears fell from my eyes and he took my hands and pulled me to my feet to hold me close to his chest.

"Tell me what troubles you."

"If you do not know, how can I tell you?" I sobbed. Putting me away from him, he looked into my face.

"You are life itself to me dearest Frances and it hurts me to see you sad. I love you so much; can it be that you are learning to love me a little?

"I have loved you for so long, long before we married."

"You love me? But I didn't know. I thought one day, you may grow to love me but wanted to give you time. You are so young and innocent and I am so many years your senior. I did not want to spoil things by rushing you."

"I have so longed for you to come to me and my thoughts have not been innocent."

The hot colour rushed to my face and I hid in his shirt. Then his mouth covered mine and I could feel his heat and longing. A fire cracker burst inside me as joy and warmth flooded my body making my legs tremble. He murmured against my cheek,

"If you only knew the nights I have paced the floor to keep myself from coming up here, you would perhaps have saved my agony. Tonight I will join you here if I may and we will be lovers. Are you sure this is what you want? There will be no turning back."

I touched his cheek,

"Yes Robert I am sure. I have never been more sure of anything."

"Come dearest heart, we shall be late for the concert. I think you will play like an angel tonight. All my love went into writing that piece, could you feel it?"

"Yes, I will play only for you tonight, not for the mayor and his lady and all the dignitaries."

September 1st. I am a woman and a wife at last. I am so ignorant; I did not know what to do but my body did under Robert's hands. He pleased me before himself so I did not mind the pain. Sometimes he is like a tiger unleashed and is fierce and powerful, at others he is gentle and tender, but always loving. My heart will burst with love for him. I am impatient for him to come to me now, but he is talking to Mr. Elliott. Eleanor and I excused ourselves. I do not trust Mr. Elliott. I think him false. He tries to charm me but treats me strangely. He looks at Eleanor in a strange way too.

December 24th. Robert has bought a charming cottage for me. I asked him not to put it in my name but in that of our child or children. Mr. Elliott is Robert's solicitor but he knows nothing of this and Robert has promised not to tell him. Robert is distressed that I do not trust Mr. Elliott but I cannot help it, there is something evil and wolfish about that man. He makes my skin crawl.

We escape to our cottage as often as possible, we make love there and I feel I have something of my very own. I am just a lodger in Robert's house, Eleanor is the mistress there and Robert understands that.

March 12th. 1866.

Today I am nineteen, a happy fulfilled woman. I hope I do not become pregnant yet, I do not want anything to change what Robert and I share. We have such fun and enjoy each other so well and heartily and as often as possible. Eleanor asked where we disappear to on slack days. I told her we have favourite places to stay and friends to stay with. I do not think Robert will give us away; our privacy is too precious to him. She does not miss us in the afternoons as we were rarely home then, now we hurry to our cottage, impatient for each other.

December 25th. Robert has bought me a diamond necklace with matching bracelet and earrings. When I protested I have so much, he said,

"I am trying to make you feel secure. If anything happens to me, you can sell these for cash if you ever need to. There is a safe with your own lawyer and he has the deeds to this cottage. Do you feel safer now?"

He has taken me to a young friendly lawyer and explained that even if I marry again these are my property alone and nobody can take them from me. I gave Robert my humble present and told him that I may be with child. My monthly bleed is a week overdue.

March 12th. 1867. I am twenty today and looking forward to the birth of our baby in August. It is a surprise there was no earlier evidence of our constant loving. Robert looks so content and indulged. He thinks I should give up playing but I do not think that at all necessary, I would have to stay home with Eleanor and see less of Robert. It does not harm us to sit on a chair and play.

August 8th. Our son Robert Francis was born this morning. We both insisted Robert should stay with me, armed guards could not have dragged him away, I was hanging on so tightly. Robert held baby Robert first then passed him to me to nurse. Young Doctor Mike did not mind but the nurse was shocked and horrified and suggested I have a wet nurse. Robert just laughed and told her,

"My wife is a trifle unconventional and has waited a long time for our baby."

The tears were running down his face as he watched us and the little chap knew just what he wanted. Poor nurse does not know I came from a farming district where the country folk follow nature.

September 14th. Our baby is thriving wonderfully but Eleanor keeps urging me to have a wet nurse so I can return to the orchestra. She thinks to take over our baby but I guard him every moment. Life is different now because Robert is apart from me so much. In a few weeks I shall take our baby with us and begin rehearsals again. I wonder whether Mrs. Askew would be interested in staying with young Robbie some evenings if Robert wishes me to play. Robert laughs at me but I can sense evil around us in this house. Why? From whom?

December 30th. Robert and I with our little son have spent the weekend here in our cottage and our loving has recommenced as vigorously as before. We shall make up some story to explain our absence. Robert is not happy about my returning to the orchestra but is pleased Mrs. Askew will stay with baby Robbie and it will not be every evening as before, maybe just one or two to begin with. I already take the child with me to rehearsals on four mornings and this works very well. Eleanor keeps on asking why I do not allow her to care for him sometimes, but she does not even like holding him and the child screams whenever she does, so I know he would be in the care of the servants and I do not want that. It is better my way.

Our loyal old butler has been replaced by a surly individual; Eleanor says Wicks was too old for the job and Thorne will be more efficient. Wicks was certainly frail but had been with the family many years. What will become of him? I shall go round to see him one day next week. I trust nobody.

March 13th. 1868. Robert gave a large party for my twenty-first Birthday yesterday. It was our fourth wedding anniversary a few days ago so it was a double celebration. David and Clarissa came and many of our orchestra friends and of course Mr. Elliott and Eleanor.

Clarissa is expecting their first child in a few weeks and David is very caring of her. Robert has bought me a beautiful gold pendant watch and chain. More in my safety deposit box. I keep them all there and take whatever I want out to wear, then replace it. Mr. Weston, my lawyer, has an office farther up the road from our cottage. He holds the keys and will release them to nobody but myself. I seem to have lived with this oppressive gloom for ever and I am certain it emanates from Mr. Elliott. He cannot harm me can he? Why should he wish to?

I found out where Wicks was living with his sister and went to see him to take him a small present. He was pleased to see me and grateful for the money. He told me that Mr. Elliott informed him he was no longer needed and Miss Eleanor was with him. He begged me to take care of the Master, he is afraid for him and for all of us. He said,

"That Mr. Elliott is a nasty piece of work and Miss Eleanor is in his power."

It is not only me then that distrusts that man!

August 8th. It is one year since our son was born and he took his first steps today. It has been a happy day. Rehearsal this morning. Went to the cottage this afternoon. Robert and I are still as much in love as ever and just as lusty in our loving. Letter from David today. His little boy is not progressing as he should. They have christened him Robert the same as our son.

<u>January 6th 1869.</u> What a busy Christmas season, so many engagements. I have played solos ten nights in two weeks. Mrs. Askew has been kept busy. Robert has taken another woman into the orchestra, a middle aged violinist of considerable skill. He says other famous orchestras are beginning to look at women as members. Of course, the more the safer.

<u>February15th.1869.</u> Robert was very ill in the night. He dined with Mr. Elliott at his house. There was some business to discuss and he stayed for a meal. This was unusual. Business topics are discussed here at lunch times never at Mr. Elliott's and never in the evening. Robert had griping pains in his stomach and was

vomiting and rolling in the bed with agony. I roused Thorne who went to bring the Doctor. He gave him some medicine which relieved him enormously. It was young Doctor Mike and he asked a lot of questions. Where had he been, what did he eat and did I eat the same food? I asked him

"What do you think has caused Robert to be so ill so suddenly Doctor?"

He replied carefully,

"These are the symptoms of arsenic poisoning Mrs. Brentwood. I would advise you to eat together at all times and to be careful. If you follow my instructions, I think he will recover but I will require a sample of his excreta in this jar, for testing. I have no proof you understand?"

<u>February 24th.</u> Robert did recover but was very shaky and weak for several days. I sent off the sample for Doctor Mike. When he was well enough I told him what Doctor Mike said but he just smiled and said,

"Then I must put my house in order my dearest."

He said Mr. Elliott and he ate the same food except for a little sugar on the fruit and Mr. Elliott did not take sweet things. Thank goodness he is better. I shall guard him with my life.

<u>July 5th.</u> Robert has taken on a deputy conductor for the orchestra and works him hard. Mr. Frankish seems a good fellow, plays organ and trumpet.

Robert has made a new will. Mr. Elliot and Mrs. Askew were witness. The document says that Robert's share in this house shall be left for his son and heir and that all of his estate shall be held by me in trust for his children but the interest from the estate shall be mine annually. In the event of both our deaths, Robbie would inherit everything. Well it sounds simple enough. Eleanor shall continue to maintain the house and servants from the moneys left her by their Father for this purpose.

<u>September 8th.</u> Robert has seemed preoccupied of late and is himself only when with baby Robbie and myself. I asked him what was worrying him, but he said it was nothing. I do not believe him. He came home one day last week from morning rehearsal; he often walks when we are not with him. Some ruffians;

robbers he suspects, set upon him, knocked him to the ground and were beating him about the head. Some workmen came out of a nearby yard to help him and the robbers ran off, but my poor Robert was badly bruised and shaken.

<u>December 30th.</u> My beloved husband, my lover and protector, Robert is dead. He was killed by a runaway carriage while walking from his coach to the rehearsal hall. He was brought here and young Doctor Mike came, but he died two hours later holding my hand. The Doctor asked me why I did not send a sample when Robert was ill. I was most surprised as I gave the sample in a package to Patty the very next day. Doctor Mike said it did not arrive and he assumed I was

unable to collect it. I feel as though I were in a net and it is tightening around me. What will I do without my darling protector?

January 2nd.1870 Robert was buried today. I feel so alone, bereft and afraid.

January 10th. Mr. Elliott called to see me today. He took me into the library and held the will in his hands. I was filled with dread.

CHAPTER THIRTEEN

When Leonard went up to bed I sneaked a quick look at the journal to find out what happened in the library. It felt a little like playing Cluedo with who killed somebody in the library with which weapon, or reading Miss Marples. I couldn't go to bed without knowing what happened next in the life of this amazing woman.

**

"Sit down Frances my dear. I have a proposition to put to you. Under the terms of Robert's last will, you are a rich woman. Now, I suggest you marry me as soon as possible so that I can look after you and your interests. In fact it is all arranged for the day after tomorrow."

I was thoroughly stunned. My mouth gaped like a fish,

"Marry you? Never. Are you mad? How dare you suggest such a thing? It is outrageous and obscene."

"I have always admired you and I think you will be sensible. This marriage will be good for my image and your safety. You see--- if you do not marry me, I shall take away your son."

"That is kidnap. You cannot do that."

"Frances, I can and I will do it. Where is he now, do you know?"

"Of course I know. He is with Mrs. Askew in the nursery."

"Well, he may be now, but you cannot guard him every moment and I can take him by force any time I choose. I will give you until tomorrow at this time when I shall require your compliance."

His hand reached out and touched my face. My skin crawled in revulsion and I jumped back. He smiled that twisted smile of his that leaves his eyes cold. He whispered,

"Until tomorrow Frances my dear."

I flew up the stairs, two at a time and burst into the nursery, where Mrs. Askew was calmly dressing my Robbie.

"Why Frances dear, you look as though you have seen a ghost. Whatever is the matter?"

"Oh Mrs. Askew, Mr. Elliott said was I sure I knew where Robbie was. He wants to take him from me."

"He can do that over my dead body dearie. You can call on me anytime."

"He is going to try and force me to marry him. Mrs. Askew, can you take Robbie home with you? If anybody tries to stop you going out of the house, say you are taking him for a walk. Keep him at your house until I come for him. If we can get Robbie away, this man will lose his power."

"Bless you now, of course I will, he will be safe with me the little love."

We finished dressing the child quickly; Mrs. Askew put on her cloak and bonnet and went down stairs carrying Robbie. I listened from the landing and heard a commotion. There were men's voices, the screams of the child and Mrs. Askew's raised voice. Running down the stairs I found Mr. Elliott clutching the howling Robbie who held out his arms when he saw me.

"Mamma, Mamma," he screamed.

My heart pounded with fear as I asked,

"What is going on here? Why is Robbie not out for his walk with Mrs. Askew?"

"Oh you knew? Thorne here caught that woman attempting to kidnap the boy and rightly called me. I intercepted her and rescued your son." He shook the screaming boy.

"She will not be coming again. She is not a suitable person to be responsible for the child. Eleanor has engaged a nanny to care for him until after our wedding my dear."

The resisting Mrs Askew was pushed out of the door by Thorne, protesting that she would bring a constable.

"You evil brute! You cannot make me marry you. I will not. You can have all the money and my part of the house and Robbie and I will go and live with my brother."

Smirking and shaking his head he responded,

"Oh dear me no. It is not that simple Frances my dear. You remember the will? The half of this house and Robert's money belong to the boy. It is not yours to hand over."

A pert girl I had not seen before, dressed in the uniform of a nanny appeared and took the still screaming form of my son and was walking towards Eleanor's parlour. I attempted to snatch the child but Mr. Elliott restrained me. The last sight I had of Robbie, was his tearful little face contorted with rage and with arms outstretched to me, looking over the girl's shoulder as they passed through the door.

"You cannot mean to go through with this insane scheme Mr. Elliott. I shall go and find a constable this minute."

These brave words met with laughter from my enemy.

"I fear you are distraught and not thinking clearly dear heart. You are a prisoner in this house until such time as we are married. All the staff and Eleanor are involved and under strict orders. You are far too sensible to do anything rash because we have the boy. He will be restored to you unharmed after the ceremony. I shall place him in an orphanage if you do not comply. Do not mistake my sentiments. He is nothing to me. I suggest you return to your suite and prepare yourself for our wedding."

Taking my frozen hands he pulled me towards him and forcefully kissed my stiff lips. Such waves of revulsion and loathing swept over me that I snatched away my hand and slapped his face.

"That was not very kind my dear, but I like a woman with spirit, I shall enjoy teaching you to submit."

There was a banging on the door and Thorne was summoned to open it. Elliott had me pinned in his arms and I could hear a man's voice outside.

"This person has complained that her mistress is being kept here a prisoner. Is the master at home, I would like to speak with him please."

Elliott whispered in my ear,

"If you want to see your son alive again, you had better keep your mouth shut and play my game Madam."

He pulled open the door and with his arm around my waist said to the Constable on the step,

"Mrs Brentwood has suffered a great shock in losing her husband and is very upset. I have sent this person away as she is a bad influence. Mrs Brentwood will tell you herself that she is not a prisoner is that not right my dear?"

I nodded dumbly.

"There is no problem Constable thank you."

"Well if you are sure Madam we will say no more about it."

Mrs Askew was screaming beside him.

"Ask to see the child Constable. They are both prisoners. Ask him."

"Now lady you are causing a nuisance. First you say it is Madam that is a prisoner now you say it is the child. That is enough. Away with you."

He dragged her down the steps.

I ran upstairs and shut myself in my rooms. Sitting by the window, I attempted to arrange my thoughts into some kind of order. This fiend had all the power. He was determined on this course to get his hands on the money and property. Where did that leave Robbie? As I saw it, he was in acute danger because although Elliott could administer the estate while Robbie was a minor, he could only own it through me in the event of

Robbie's death or---if we were all out of the way. The realization of this implication hit me like a hammer. Robbie was in grave danger, perhaps not now but when it suited Mr. Elliott. My beloved Robert made a will that was a death sentence for Robbie and me.

Who were our allies? The Askews, David, Mr. Weston and maybe Doctor Mike Saunders. These were the only people I could fully trust, but how could they help us now? Mr. Elliot held all the trump cards and he knew it.

CHAPTER FOURTEEN

The next morning saw the three of us packed into our car with two cellos, music stand, Charlie’s gown for her recital and numerous other necessities. The journal was secured in its box on my lap. We found the address easily and were welcomed into the house by Robert and his wife Elizabeth. Entering their sitting room, we were introduced to a tall fair young man of athletic build. Although I was prepared for it, his likeness to Charlie and to the picture was quite remarkable and uncanny. His hair was a warm gold colour, lighter than Charlies, the fearless violet blue eyes sparkled beneath the same arched brows but the pointed nose was more masculine, the chin squarer and more determined. He bore no resemblance to his mother’s slight build and dark colouring or to his father. Where Elizabeth’s hair was straight and worn in a smart bob, young Robert’s was a mass of tight curls slightly longer than a short back and sides.

“This is Rob our son, Jean our daughter was married last year and lives in Worcester. She was visiting the day you first phoned and it was she who answered.”

Fran made introductions.

"This is my husband Len and this is our daughter Charlotte but known as Charlie. She will be dashing away to her appointment in a few minutes."

The meeting between this Rob of theirs and our Charlie was how I imagine being caught in an electric storm would feel. Each appraised the other as would combatants in a ring, weighing the potential, taking a measure. I could imagine the crackle of sparks and the smell of sulphur. Was it imagination that brought into my mind the certainty these two would either love or hate with great intensity? They would certainly meet again.

They were thrown together almost immediately as we enjoyed coffee and the position was explained. Charlie needed transport into Manchester for her Saturday afternoon appointment and would take our car which grounded us until the evening. Rob then volunteered to drive her and the instruments, because he was giving a lecture at the college in the city and their times and venues were compatible. Rob was shown the old cello before it was loaded into the back of his battered Volvo estate. He expressed amazement on seeing the wonderful condition of the aged instrument saying as he stroked the wood,

"Somebody has cared to this treasure for many years. It's a gem. Must drive carefully!"

After they left us, Robert showed us their sprawling garden, a surprising mixture of the riotous colour of competing plants, shrubs and the tranquil peace of cool, shady arbours.

"Elizabeth is responsible for the design and flower beds and the veg patch is my domain."

Robert told us with a chuckle,

"You will note there are more weeds in my part than hers. This you understand is because she has more time to play than me."

Elizabeth gave him a playful push on his arm and retaliated,

"The real truth is I am better organized and not into family history like some folk."

The rivalry was all in fun and obviously ongoing. Later the four of us strolled to the pub on the corner and had a leisurely lunch. During this, I apologetically confessed to Robert I had not yet finished the journal but brought it along in the hope of being allowed to keep it longer.

"Of course. There is no problem but you understand why I make it a rule to keep it in sight. You are family and perhaps closer than you realize yet?"

"Well, the thought has occurred to me once or twice that maybe our Frances could be pregnant again before her husband died."

Robert was enjoying a succulent steak and paused mid forkful to stare at me in amazement,

"You haven't yet read that far?"

I answered his surprised query with a shake of my head and he continued,

"How on earth did you guess? It never occurred to me."

Smiling at his incredulous expression I told him,

"Firstly I'm a woman. Secondly, I think it was when I began to touch and read the journal, the thought fell into my head. Then it recurred when I saw the picture and when I met your Rob. They could not resemble each other so strongly if too many different genes were involved. Reading the journal is like reading Charlie's character; she is so like that Frances in disposition and looks. They appear to share the same courage and tenacity as well as talent."

On our return Leonard and Elizabeth sat in the garden comparing plants and chatting, while Robert took me into his den to show the journal he was compiling. This featured his discoveries about our ancestors, his parents and grandparents lives. The beautiful miniature from which my copy was taken, was hanging on the wall beneath the book-shelves away from strong, damaging daylight. It was held in the original, exquisite, heavy carved silver frame.

Robert's own family account was the work of time and much painstaking research. There were present day photos of the vicarage where Frances spent her childhood, the old hall of Squire Porter, the town mansion house of Robert the conductor. This latter was a copy from an old history journal. A large head and shoulder picture of this Robert holding his baton copied from the same journal. There was an announcement copied from an old Manchester Guardian of

'Mr. Francis Brown playing a cello.'

A further cutting showed a picture of Frances now as his wife.

'The music written by Mr. Robert Brentwood to celebrate their marriage. '

An advertisement from the same newspaper to the effect that,

> 'At the next concert of the New Orchestra, Miss Frances Brown, wife of the conductor Robert Brentwood, will play a solo written by Mr Brentwood and dedicated to his wife.'

There was some documentation, a family tree, birth, marriage and death certificates, census returns, a picture of Hannah Frances as a small child with a baby in long clothes, taken in 1871. This was the baby Charles Elliott, third child of Frances. A picture of a child of perhaps three years sitting, was unnamed. Robert thought this was almost certainly his Gt. Grandfather Robert Francis Brentwood, Robbie of the journal, but there was no proof of that as there was no inscription on the back, just a faded date 1871. Taking from her bag a photograph of the old cello and bow, Fran said,

"Here is one more to swell your collection."

"Thank you, this will copy well. I have made two copies of everything so both Jean and Rob have a history of their Family. Jean has no interest as yet but there will come a day when she wants to know her roots."

"This is all fascinating and gives me lots of ideas on compiling my own journal along similar lines. If you would like copies of my incomplete family tree, I am more than happy to share. In return I appreciate your tree and eventually we can work out the two families which have Frances Brown as a root."

The room used as a den was lined with books on family history and history local to Manchester, early days of the Orchestra and other interesting titles. There was a fiche reader, files, papers, a computer and printer and other paraphernalia jostling for space on the desk. Fran felt really at home there.

"You know, I could lose myself in here for a week without surfacing."

"Frances, I really am delighted to meet and know you and I am so pleased you put that ad. in the Family Tree magazine. If I'd placed one some years ago, you wouldn't have seen it I suppose?"

"No, but my friend Amy might have. It was through her that I began looking and she has guided me along."

Robert showed me how he was transcribing some memorial inscriptions that members of his society recorded from gravestones in cemeteries. He used the computer for this and put the information on to disks after which it was double checked and put on to fiche. Other society members could request information from these or any other fiche and copies were sold. This way knowledge was shared between societies and counties and was especially useful for people trying to research their ancestors from a distance.

"Of course things are moving on rapidly and more info is becoming available on the internet. I suspect we will very soon be able to access the early census returns that way. For some it will make searching so much easier and less laborious."

Suddenly the voice of Elizabeth from downstairs announced six-o-clock, tea and the return of Rob and Charlie. The concert was well received and Charlie earned a standing ovation for the 'Little Nocturne'. Flushed with success, eyes alight and sparkling with mischief, animation bubbling from every pore, her face betrayed an inner excitement. Rob sitting over the table from her was drawn into her orbit and the ensuing repartee bounced from side to side like a ping-pong ball, infecting the rest of us, inviting our witty contributions. Robert's eyes met mine across the table and we exchanged smiles. It was a light-hearted meal, full of promise. Charlie solved the problem of returning the journal by saying she was in Manchester again in two weeks if she could be trusted to drop off the precious parcel.

"Don't worry Dad, my car will be on the road again by then if I can pay the garage bill."

Opinions on the day were thrown around on the journey home; the new relatives being out of hearing were discussed freely and met with general approval. The precious journal was once more safely in Fran's clutches and she intended burning the midnight oil to find out more.

CHAPTER FIFTEEN

February 4th.1870 I am desolate, a helpless woman in a house of evil. My heart aches for my little one, I can hear his cries all the time. Is it in my mind? There is no escape for me. There are two large bedrooms in my suite, with a communicating door that has been locked from the other side. All morning there was great activity in the next room. When I asked what was going on there, the servants said they had orders to clean and prepare it for use. I was very angry but could learn no more.

Mr. Elliott came to see me this afternoon to tell me that plans for our marriage are complete and there will be just a small wedding breakfast with a few influential friends of his. I asked why my brother could not be present and was told that he would be able to visit afterwards but only with Mr. Elliott present. He said,

"David ceased to be responsible for you when you married Robert and we do not want him causing any trouble do we?"

I asked why he did not marry Eleanor instead of me but he laughed and replied scornfully;

"My dear Frances, I thought you more intelligent and observant. Eleanor and I have been lovers for years but when I marry you, I can have all that is yours too and enjoy her and what is hers. The best of both worlds as it were."

I then asked why none of my Robert's friends or orchestra

colleagues were invited. He simply snapped,

"That should be obvious to you Frances. They would ask too many questions so is best to keep quiet."

As he was leaving the room Elliott leered evilly then looked over his shoulder to say,

"By the way, if you are wondering about your second room, Eleanor is moving in there so that I am more easily able to move between rooms. This will greatly enhance the pleasure and enjoyment in store for us all."

As his meaning became clear, horror and disgust filled me. I cannot believe anybody capable of such depravity. This monster is even more despicable than I thought and is moving his mistress into the next room. I have never liked nor understood Eleanor but did not suspect her of such duplicity. Perhaps he has some hold over her too. My poor Robert, to be surrounded by such vipers. Did he know they were lovers? Did he partly suspect something? Is that why he insisted I have my own cottage and lawyer and why he gave me so many valuables? They are of little use while I am a prisoner here, but one day there will be a chance, he cannot always guard me.

There is a new gown hanging in my room for tomorrow and he says I must always be well dressed because of his prestige and to show the public how happy we are. I will only be allowed to play solo with the Orchestra so that he can enjoy the limelight and always accompany me. Robert, oh my

Robert, I miss you so. My heart is breaking and I am so alone.

February 5th. This is my wedding morning, my day of doom. Forgive me my darling for what I am about to do. I have no choice. It is either this or lose our child.

February 12th. My life is more unbearable than I thought life could be. Every day is a burden with fresh horrors. My only consolation, that I have my Robbie back with me. At first he fought and kicked me but I soon recovered him by gentle talk and loving. I dread to think what has happened to him. There are many bruises on his little body and he is very thin and frightened.

I had not thought Mr. Elliott would need or demand his conjugal rights. How naïve I was and how mistaken. When I refused him the first night he said,

"My dear Frances have you still not realized why you are in this position? You will give me a son because I require an heir and you will fulfil your wifely duties until this is accomplished."

Eleanor was then called to disrobe me while he calmly undressed. Then in front of her he attacked me. The more I kicked, screamed and hit him, the more he laughed and the more excited he became. When I was completely overpowered, she sat naked on the floor beside him, stroking his back while he ravished my body. This has since continued repeatedly, night and morning. I am exhausted and fearful. He is a brutal, sadistic deviant and constantly finds new obscenities to inflict upon me whether alone or in the presence of Eleanor, little Robbie or even on one occasion, the upstairs maid who stayed to enjoy the show. I do not suppose Eleanor alone satisfied him before, a harem could not satisfy him. His sexual appetite and behaviour is perverted and insatiable, he enjoys the pain and degradation he forces upon me. He ties me face down over a chair and beats me with a strap then bites and pinches my body where it is not seen, before raping me brutally. I hope he does no harm to my little secret, the only other part of my beloved Robert left to me except Robbie. How soon before I dare tell him, so that he will leave me alone. He must think he put it there or neither of us will be safe.

February 20th. I told him when he came into my room tonight that my bleeding is overdue almost a week and suspect I am with child. For my reward I was dragged into Eleanor's room by the hair and given a demonstration of how real pleasure was taken and given. I was appalled and quite nauseated but thank heavens he did not touch me. Is that nightmare finally over? He is to ask the Doctor to confirm, just in case I am trying to put him off!

February 27th. Young Doctor Mike visited but Mr. Elliott insisted on being present.

"Where is old Doctor Saunders? We always use him."

"My father is often ill and I do a lot of his work now." He lifted my gown at the back to listen to my lungs and asked,

"What are the scars Mrs Elliot?"

Quick as flash Mr. Elliott answered for me,

"She was beaten as a child. Get on with what you are here for."

Doctor Mike saw the marks on my wrists where I have been bound but made no comment, just looked at me. I cannot cry or give anything away. He must have seen the other marks on my body too but stayed silent.

"How is little Robbie Mrs Elliott, he must be a big boy now."

"He is very well, thank you Doctor, chatters all the time. Mr.Elliott will you call Robbie please, I am sure Doctor Mike would like to see him."

Mr. Elliott glared at me malevolently but went to the door and called the maid. Doctor Mike whispered,

"How far pregnant do you want to be Mrs. Elliott?"

"About three weeks Doctor Mike, since February 5th."

"Can I do anything for you, take a message perhaps?"

Shaking my head I whispered,

"Nobody can help me."

Mr.Elliott was back at my side.

"Tell the Askews you have found me well if you meet, I have not seen them for a few weeks."

"I will indeed Mrs Elliott."

As Mr Elliott approached dragging a terrified Robbie by the hand he continued,

"Oh hello, so this is young Robbie. He is a fine boy and looks healthy."

Robbie cowered away from Mr. Elliott and ran over to me. That gentleman looked sour and remarked,

"It is time he was weaned away from his mother and a new baby is just the thing to do it, don't you think Doctor?"

"I think he is just a baby himself Mr.Elliott and needs his mother's love for a long time yet." Mr Elliott glowered at him but Doctor Mike continued calmly.

"There are early signs suggesting a pregnancy and from what you have told me, your symptoms point in that direction. No positive signs to confirm this at present. May I suggest you rest a lot and sleep alone for the next few weeks, so that nothing disturbs the foetus at this critical stage? I would like you to look into my office in four weeks time for a further check-up. I could possibly work out a date then for your confinement. Good day to you and to you Mr. Elliott."

When he left, Mr. Elliott stormed,

"That fellow is impertinent and what was he whispering to you?"

"He just asked me whether I recognized any symptoms."

"Mm. That was very sly of you to mention Mrs. Askew. He pinched the skin on my breast between finger and thumb and nipped hard then screwed a hand in my hair to force my head back while he took my hand and forced me to fondle him. Then he roughly kissed and bit my mouth hard. Mr. Elliott's parting words were,

"You will need to be very careful dear Frances, just

remember how easy it is to take your boy. However you may have a few weeks to anticipate resuming your wifely duties. You will enjoy my lovemaking much more after being deprived for a while and I have thought of new ways to amuse and pleasure you."

My poor little Robbie who has known nothing but gentleness and laughter in his young life, to witness the savagery of this animal.

March 14th. David came to visit without warning this afternoon, I suppose they thought he would ask questions if he was not allowed to see me. Mr. Elliott was present and introduced himself as my new husband. David was refused permission to speak to me alone, as Mr.Elliott said,

"Anything that concerns my beloved Frances, concerns me too."

David asked when I last saw Mrs. Askew and I replied truthfully that it was two days before our marriage. David then asked if I would like to bring Robbie to stay with him and Clarissa for a day or two and see how wonderfully their baby was coming on in spite of his handicaps. Mr. Elliott said he could not permit that as the Doctor had just confirmed the strong possibility I may be with child and the travelling would be harmful just now. David sat beside me and took my hand,

"You look exhausted and ill Frances, are you sure everything is well with you? You will tell me if something is worrying you?"

I felt the tears rush into my eyes as I looked at him helplessly. David knows me very well and I am certain he could read distress in my face, then he looked down at my wrists where he could not fail to see the bruises.

"Everything is in order David dear; I will come to visit you and Clarissa to check on my little nephew as soon as Mr.Elliott says I may."

June 10th. Mr Elliott took me to see Doctor Mike at his office this morning and stayed for the examination. Doctor Mike says everything is in order and the child is growing. He expects me to give birth in early November. Witnessing all this excited Mr Elliott who could not wait to take me upstairs to bed but pushed me into the library and raped me there. I have learned to take it silently. My tormentor is taking his pleasure regularly once more. He says he has obeyed the Doctor and I need his attentions to give him a healthy son. The degrading acts are too disgusting to record.

<u>September 19. 1870.</u> My beautiful little daughter was born last week, very tiny and totally unlike Robbie when he was born. Thankfully she is perfect and healthy despite the rough treatment of the past few days and nobody suspects. I would fear for her life if there was any doubt about her father being Mr. Elliott. Doctor Mike noticed all my bruises. He stayed with me the whole time and would allow nobody but his nurse in and her not all the time. Mr. Elliott is squeamish in this kind of situation; I find this totally out of character and laughable. In

between times, Doctor Mike coaxed the whole story from me and said he had spoken to the Askews and so had David. My brother is very worried and concerned since his visit and confided his worries to the Askews.

Dr Mike said

"I understand now the hold Mr. Elliott has over you and how he forced you into this marriage. If there is anything at all that I can do to aid your escape from this prison, you can count on me and your other friends, but you will have to choose the time. We do not wish to cause you further problems."

My mixed feelings at seeing the child and learning she is a girl instead of the anticipated boy overwhelmed me and I sobbed out my anguish.

"Mrs Elliott, this child is beautiful and her lightweight makes her seem early. Why are you so upset at this time?"

"Mr. Elliott needs a son to inherit from him Doctor Mike. Can you imagine what that means for me?"

Doctor Mike again expressed his willingness to help in any way he could and told me that the Askews are aware of the situation and how worried they and my brother are about me.

"Mr. Askew passes this house at eleven o clock each morning and pauses outside the next house but one, if there is any way you could get a message to him, he is willing and ready to help."

"Thank them for me Doctor Mike, I never cease to look for an opportunity to escape but it will be even more difficult now, with two babies."

<u>November 7th.</u> My nightmare has resumed, Mr. Elliott

demanded his marital rights when my beautiful Hannah Frances was just two weeks old and he pursues his pleasures with more bestial brutality than formerly. I expect he is punishing me for needing an interlude as if he was not gratified elsewhere. I cannot help but overhear the romps that go on the other side of the wall. Sometimes it sounds as though there are several people frolicking about in the next room and that would not surprise me. He gives dinner parties and never ceases to humiliate and degrade me before guests but I suspect they are as bad as him. I have to sit beside him and he forces me to wear the most revealing dresses so that he can paw me for all to see. The guests are almost all men and Eleanor appears to enjoy their attentions. One evening halfway through the meal, one of the loathsome creatures dragged her from the room and they returned when the meal was almost finished looking half dressed and dishevelled. She is nothing better that a whore. If Mr.Elliott did not want a son so badly, I am sure he would be letting me out to the highest bidder. That is probably what he has in mind for my future when I have fulfilled my obligations. I shall kill myself first.

November 21st. I played solo last night at the request of Mr.Frankish and had to disguise a huge bite on my neck, bruised arms and a bruise on my cheek, nor could I sit comfortably for hurting. They watch me all the time and go everywhere with me, there is no chance to escape. How can I bear this, but I must for my babies.

December 7th. I suspect I may once again be with child, I feel so sick and ill and never have before. I had to start giving my baby some solid food to satisfy her until I feel better. I told Mr. Elliott to leave me alone unless he wants me to miscarry. He flew into a rage and forced me to perform acts of obscenity upon his body before he went off to Eleanor's room. It made me physically sick but I will do anything if he will just leave me alone. This is the depth of depravity to which I have sunk. As soon as this child is born, please

God make it a boy, I must get away with my babies. I am afraid for Robbie. I try to keep him out of harm's way but it is not always possible to prevent him seeing the atrocious things Mr. Elliott does to me. Things he should not see, nobody should especially not a child of four.

February 16th. I am feeling better and have begun to take a more definite interest in the routine of the house members now the sickness has passed. Mr. Elliott goes to business at 10A.M. returning at 2 P.M. Eleanor floats in and out at all times, but is always out on Tuesday mornings. I am permitted to take Robbie out at 11 A.M. for a walk, always accompanied by a manservant. I am not allowed to take baby Hannah with us. We go across to the park and play on the grass and feed the ducks. There are various visitors to the house, Eleanor's friends, strange people, and Mr. Elliott's business associates.

Tradesmen always use the rear entrance and ring a bell at the gate. There is a garden here but it is surrounded by a high wall and the gate is locked and bolted. There is no escape that way as the rear door goes outside from the kitchen. I shall find a way. I must. I don't think my little Robbie will be safe if this child is a boy. They will not need him any more.

August 1st. The child was born last night, Mr. Elliott has his son and is delighted as am I. I feel like a brood mare. The child looks like a frog and I can feel nothing for it but aversion. He is making me nurse it but has employed a nanny again.

CHAPTER SIXTEEN

It was midnight and Leonard was going up to bed as he put his head around the door of the sitting room.

"Are you coming to bed Fran? It's past midnight and we have an early start in the morning"

"She is just about to plot her escape so I can't leave her just yet. Be up shortly dear."

The following day we were making a visit to Thomas and Janet to see the progress of our granddaughter. Leonard had picked the soft fruit to freeze and I did a big bake, most of which was also frozen. We were taking with us a cooked chicken and fruit pies. It was like a busman's holiday but the time we would spend with them would give us further opportunity of cementing our relationship with Janet and getting to know baby Bethany.

**

September 16th. 1891. I am free with my babies, but have left Mr. Elliott's son behind. I was becoming quite attached to him, poor little creature and wonder what will become of him. It was either him or us but I could not risk any harm coming to my little Robbie and I am sure it was intended.

I chose a Tuesday when I knew Eleanor would be out visiting. In the end, escape was so easy I wonder why I did not attempt it last year after Hannah was born, except they have been less vigilant of late. I am sure they did not think I would desert the baby. My plans were made with the help of Doctor Mike who told Mr. Askew to be ready on a Tuesday around 11 A.M. when I hoped to be taking Hannah and Robbie for their walk with my body guard. I was to wave a white cloth from my window the morning before if the plan was to proceed. This all went smoothly. I had recommenced our walks a week earlier and was feeling reasonably well since my confinement. I strapped my journal around my middle and dressed myself and the children in a double layer of clothes. We took nothing with us to arouse suspicion and walked to the park as usual. Mr. Elliott was at his offices and Eleanor was occupied with her usual visiting. I was terrified that something unforeseen would occur to stop us.

The weather was lovely and we just walked out of the door and along the pavement as though it was an ordinary day. A carriage passed us and pulled up a few houses along the road. As we reached it a man jumped Thorne our bodyguard from behind, gagging him. Mr. Askew leaped from the carriage and together they heaved the stunned man up on to the top seat. We were bundled inside where my beloved Mrs. Askew was waiting for us. The children were frightened but she was so good with them, that all was soon calm and I think Robbie remembered her a little. My whole body shook with the suddenness of it. All I could think of was our freedom and putting as much distance between us and that house as possible, as fast as the horses could go.

"What will happen to the footman?"
I asked and was told,

"Mr. Askew will dump him in the bushes, bound and gagged, further along the road. He will be quickly found."

Mrs Askew was cuddling Robbie and little Hannah and crooning her baby songs to them as she continued,

"Then we will take you to the cottage. It is not safe for you at our house; that is the first place they will look. What a task it was trying to convince that Mr. Weston of yours, it was for you and the children that I needed the cottage key. It was a good job Mr. Askew went with me as I had nothing written to show him. We both came up with the same story or he would not have given it to us and we should have to break in. As it was, he insisted on going with us to open up the place and get it aired for you and some provisions in.”

“Bless you Mrs Aiskew for all you have done. What good friends you both are.”

Gradually as we journeyed further I began to feel easier and the shaking settled. I also felt I should be feeding the baby and guilt washed over me and tears rushed to my eyes. Mrs Aiskew noticed and patted my hand.

“You must feel distressed at leaving the baby but I know Doctor Mike will keep an eye on him. We talked about you maybe having to leave him behind to rescue these little mites.”

How fortuitous that we left the spare key to the cottage with Mr. Weston, Mr. Elliott never did discover where all the keys belonged that he found on

Robert's key ring. Bless her dear heart, Mrs. Askew stayed at the cottage a few days to help settle us in and give us some confidence and security. Nobody would get past her I am quite sure, on pain of death. There were clothes to purchase for the children and myself, for we had nothing but the things we stood in.

CHAPTER SEVENTEEN

We set off early the following morning despite my being bleary eyed after reading too late and my head being full of the story of that first Frances. However it was a beautiful day and we stopped at a pub on the way for coffee before steering our way through the new road set up in Lincoln city.

In the short time since I saw her last, our small granddaughter had filled out and settled into a flexible routine. Janet was taking things in her stride now there was someone coming in to do the background chores of the domestic scene.

It was Leonard's first meeting with Bethany and he was so overwhelmed as her tiny hand curled around his finger. I'm certain I could see a tear glistening on his lashes. Janet was so grateful for everything and welcomed our offerings with delight.

"I missed you so much when you left last time and didn't tell you how much you helped me. I was so uptight and afraid of doing things wrong but your calm and assurance made it all come right."

She gave us both big warm hugs as she continued,

"Because Bethany was always hungry I thought the dairy supply was inadequate but then you told me how you remember struggling with your first baby and how anxious you were. You were right you know she just fed and fed until she was around ten pounds and since then has gone right through the night."

Janet's face was full of love and she was so proud of Bethany and how happy she was. As I watched this wonder baby sitting on my lap and staring at me, I talked to her and a wide grin spread across her little face and lit up her eyes. Both Janet and I whooped together and the boys came running.

"What's wrong?" Thomas yelped and Leonard just stared at me enquiringly.

Janet smugly replied,

"Nothing wrong, everything right. Bethany just gave her Gran a big smile. Fancy that now. I'm the one who feeds her and Gran here gets the smiles."

"Aha," Leonard crowed, "She's just putting her name down for future cherry pie."

We stayed two nights and enjoyed the intervening day as a family. Thomas was off duty from his stressful work. Although he loved working in the practice, his caseload was heavy and the work demanding. He relished the special time he spent with his girls.

We returned home on Saturday evening and on Sunday morning Charlie breezed in. Her car was now in road-worthy condition and she was, as usual, awaiting the month end and her salary cheque.

"Guess who I was with last night Mum?"

"Charlie, I lose track of your men friends. I can't guess. Hey! Wait a minute. Not Rob Brentwood?"

Her face registered amazement.

"How did you guess, are you clairvoyant?"

"No, but I did think there would be some strong attraction or repulsion between you. Was it by accident?"

"No-o, he asked for my number last weekend and rang on Wednesday to suggest we ate together last night. He is a very knowledgeable man and charming. Very likable!"

"Mm. I've never heard you so loquacious about a man before. Usually by the time they sit you across a table, you've lost interest,"

"I'm in love with him Mum, I knew as soon as we met and feel as though I've always known him."

She looked at me cautiously

"Do you think perhaps I have?"

"Maybe. It does appear that your Great Gran and his Great Granddad were sister and brother and you certainly resemble each other in looks and perhaps in temperament. You can be stubborn Charlie and I would think too, that Rob can. There will be areas where you clash, maybe violently. Can you overcome that?"

"You're right, there are bits of no man's land, but most people have those and learn to live with them. He's serious Mum. He's asked me to marry him."

"Wow! A man who knows what he wants and wastes no time. You must do as your heart tells you love, you've had plenty of choice and you're not a dewy eyed teenager. Marriage should be for keeps and has to be worked at Charlie; it's not just a legalized bed hop."

I put my arms around her and gave her a big hug.

"I know Rob is a geologist. But what does he do exactly?

"A mixture of things on a consultative basis. Oil firms and jewel companies use him for initial explorative bores and any others who require fresh fields to be tested. But he's also studied archaeology and his real love is ancient history. He goes off on those digs you read about, especially if it might be Neolithic."

“So his work must take him abroad a bit?”

“Ye-es it does and I’ll not always be able to go with him, but a lot of couples overcome that one. Look at service families.”

“Yes darling, it’s just that I want your life to be all smooth sailing and of course, life isn’t like that. You’ll work it out for yourselves.”

There wasn’t the usual gulf when Charlie left in fact for the first time I was pleased to wave her off so that I could press on with the journal.

CHAPTER EIGHTEEN

I sent for Mr. Weston and he came the next morning. He had been very concerned about us since he knew of Robert's death and heard of my remarriage. He knew something was very wrong but Robert had told him never to contact me unless I asked him. I explained our position, told him of the will and the danger I supposed my little Robbie to be in should Mr. Elliott find us. Mr. Weston assured me that the assets he held for me were safe and if anything happened to me they would pass directly to my children and then to my brother.

I asked Mr. Weston to free me from this monster and he will commence divorce proceedings immediately, citing Eleanor as respondent, charging him with marriage by force and extreme cruelty.

I told him I thought it a great shame that I am unable to prove Robert had been murdered although I was certain this was the case and they achieved success at third attempt. He was very shocked and said,

"I am aware of the reputation of Mr. Elliott and know of some very disreputable business deals in which he has been involved. I was much surprised at the marriage taking place and thought all was not well. But murder you say? Dear me, and that he should get away with it, dear me."

Mr. Weston is taking out an immediate injunction against Mr. Elliott, preventing him taking either of the children, of seeing them or me or having any contact with us, except through him. He will be breaking the law if he ever knocks upon the door. I shall be looking over my shoulder for many months to come until we are legally safe from him, but I feel easier now and the sense of freedom fills me with exhilaration. I feel years younger.

Mr. Askew has rescued my beloved cello from the orchestra and assured Mr.Frankish that I am alive and well but will not be playing with them again. I have written to David but not disclosed our whereabouts just yet. The fewer people who know, the safer I feel.

October 12th. We have moved house again. My beautiful cottage is to be sold and Mr. Weston has rented one for us near Oldham. Mr. Elliott has put out a warrant for my arrest on a charge of kidnapping his daughter and stealing family jewellery of great value. Mr. Weston feels I have less chance of being found if we move from the Manchester area. He says the charge will not stick, but to disprove it means giving away our whereabouts and it is imperative he does not find Robbie, his life would not be worth tuppence.

I asked Mr. Weston to communicate with Doctor Mike to ascertain the well being of the baby I deserted. From our position of relative safety, I am filled with guilt and remorse that I left the poor little mite in the hands of those fiends. He will have all that money can buy, but will have no mother and the evil influences upon his young character are terrifying to contemplate.

January 6th. 1892. We are now well settled in our new neighbourhood, on the outskirts of the town in a tiny village on the side farthest from Manchester. I am accepted as a young widow with her two children. I have told Robbie not to talk about Mr. Elliott because he might find us and take us back to that nasty house to live with him again. Robbie did not like Mr. Elliott and was afraid of him. I hate the need to caution him when he is just settling down, but deem it necessary.

March 3rd. Doctor Mike has written to me via Mr Weston, applauding our escape. He tells me he had to attend the child they have named Charles, because of feeding problems when we first left. He managed to find a wet nurse and the child is thriving well. The young girl left and an older kinder person is there who cares well for the child. I can imagine her opinion of the heartless mother who deserted her baby, especially when they fill her with their lies. When Doctor Mike heard about the charges against me, he was so furious he says he felt like telling Mr. Elliott he did not father Hannah, but knew he must keep the door open.

This journal is to be sent to David to hold in trust for Robbie. One day he will want to know the full story and I may not be there to tell him. Mr. Weston will see my packages are delivered safely.

The neighbours are very kind but I feel very alone and cut off from those I love and trust, I cannot risk David or anybody visiting just *yet. I worry somebody may lead them to us. There must be no evidence to show who we really are. I thank God I have my beloved cello but my heart is breaking.*

CHAPTER NINETEEN

Robert rang towards the end of that week in great excitement.

"Are you prepared for a surprise Frances?"

"You've found another journal. I've just finished reading this and feel I've been left up in the air and waiting for more."

"No, not a journal, but I found a third marriage and was certain it was her but guess who? I was so impatient I couldn't wait for a certificate through the post, so went over yesterday to collect it personally. Come on, I'll bet you can't guess who she married."

"Was it Dr. Mike?"

"Well I'm blowed. How did you guess? I thought you'd go for Mr. Weston."

"I guessed you thought it was he because you sound so surprised about your discovery which meant it couldn't be. Besides I think she had enough of the legal profession with Mr. Elliott."

"Yes you're right there. Her brother David was witness to the marriage and a couple with the same name as Dr. Mike, perhaps his brother. You remember telling me of some lady who used to visit your Grandma Hannah? What was her name?"

"Oh. You mean Aunt Becky Saunders. I never knew how she fitted into the family. It was said she was married to a soldier and lived her life in India, but I didn't hear of any family."

"Well, we may find out who she was because Dr. Mike's name was Saunders. Perhaps Frances had a son to him. We can find that out but we shall never know the whole story of her life, it's just so wonderful that we know so much about her."

"I couldn't agree more, I'm still not used to the thrill of finding you and the wonderful journal. By the way, has Rob said anything to you?"

"Rob? No. What about?"

"Did you know he and Charlie have been meeting?"

"So, that's the reason he's been on the boil all week. Well, well. I shouldn't be surprised after their electrifying first meeting. Rob was never one to bother with the ladies. He was smitten very badly as a student and hasn't seemed interested since. He's a lad who makes up his mind quickly. He sees something he wants a car, a job or whatever and goes straight for it."

"Well then, you won't be surprised if he runs true to form."

We chatted easily for a few minutes more before I mentioned a thought that was puzzling me.

"Robert, do you recall at the end of her journal, Frances says her heart is breaking but doesn't say why? I found that mystifying. She also says 'Mr. Weston delivered the packages'. Why was her heart breaking at this stage and what package besides the journal? Is it easy for you to see the census of the area where David lived, for 1881?"

"Oh yes, our library now have a copy and I can call there in the morning to check. Why? You think something else happened to her?"

"I wondered whether Frances may have sent her little Robbie to live with his uncle David for safety. If David moved nobody would know this wasn't his son, the boys had the same name, or perhaps his child died."

"That hadn't occurred to me and it would explain her remark. You're really into this family history lark now Fran. It's a bit like playing detective isn't it?"

"Mmm. It could explain why our families became separated. I've wondered about that too. People who share a family tie, usually exchange Christmas greetings at least, unless there was some disagreement."

Robert not only found little Robbie aged fourteen years, a student and living as nephew to David Brown and Clarissa but an addition in the form of Charlotte Brown, aged five years. Of their own son Robert, there was no mention, so maybe he didn't survive. That could be verified later. Robert also found the will of Charles Elliott, son of William Elliott and Frances. Charles died as a soldier in 1917, a victim of world war one. In the will, Charles bequeathed his share of the house and estate, inherited from his Aunt Eleanor Brentwood and that portion for which he was custodian on behalf of his half brother Robert Francis Brentwood. His words,

> "I leave the whole estate unconditionally to Robert Brentwood if that person can be found, to redress the wrongs inflicted by my father, the late William Elliott."

The lawyer, who drew up the will, was Hugh Weston. How Charles discovered him can only be guessed but it seems highly possible, the lawyer being Mr. Weston, that little Robbie did come into his inheritance, but the house was totally destroyed by a huge fire in 1917 around the same time as the report of Charles death.

Robert continued,

"There's a newspaper report I quote,

‘The cause of the fire has not been discovered but a body identified as that of Eleanor Brentwood, the 77 year old resident of the house, was found in a downstairs room among the debris.’

Here Robert took a deep breath before continuing,

“She probably set fire to the place for spite when she knew Charles wasn’t returning, so that Robbie couldn’t have it. I never heard of any of my family coming into money, or being wealthy so, unless like Bleak House it’s still held in Chancery, Rob will always need to earn his living.”

“Mm, maybe. We aren’t quite destitute though, there’s always the box Gran Hannah left to me with the cello. I only ever saw it once as a child, in fact I’d forgotten its existence until I mentioned it to you when we met. I need to give notice of one week to the bank to retrieve it. Would you and Elizabeth care to come over to lunch a week Sunday? That gives me plenty of time to take out the box, then we can look at the contents. I seem to remember there being a string of green beads which could be the emeralds referred to in her journal.”

“What an exciting life we do lead. We would be delighted to join you for lunch and look over the treasure.”

“I have another query.”

“Come on, let’s have it.”

“That picture I have of my Gran Hannah Frances with the soldier who I think could be Charles. If it was him, it means they must have made contact at some time. Do you think it could have been when Mr. Elliott died?”

“That’s a thought.”

Fran was still gazing at the picture of her Gran as a young woman with the young soldier. It puzzled her.

“Robert, do you think Frances somehow brought Charles to live with her maybe when she married again? How else could my Gran know him? There must be another story there.”

Robert laughed,

“Off you go again. Of course the soldier could be Mike Saunder’s son with Frances or his brother couldn’t it? We may have to await the next census to find that out. Wasn’t it your friend who said, you solve one puzzle only to create another mystery?”

“Yes it was but I don’t like being left up in the air. I shall try to find out and let you know.”

The following morning Fran set off on her cycle to the library with one thought in her head. She spent the previous evening nibbling away at the family puzzle and knew just what she would search for.

Seated at a fiche machine with film of deaths inserted she began to search for the death of William Elliott after 1871 when Charles was born. Her idea paid off. He didn’t live to a ripe old age but died in the second quarter of 1878 in Manchester.

Fran muttered under her breath,

‘Hmm. All his scheming didn’t do him any good. Horrid man.’

When Fran called to tell Amy and see what she thought, the kettle was on and coffee made in a very short time. When acquainted with this new discovery Amy said at once,

“Have you checked the 1881 census for Frances? That’s the obvious thing to do now.”

Fran gaped at her,

“Of course. Why didn’t I think of that? Robert checked it for brother David and I didn’t think to ask him to check her.”

Fran's brain was still gnawing away at the soldier photo and the puzzle it created.

"That's another trip for him as our library doesn't have a copy as yet."

"I shouldn't think it will be long before they have. Very soon we'll be able to access all the census on our home computers if we join one of the Family History sites."

Fran was impatient to get home and speak to Robert with this new information and request. He picked up at once and she heard the now familiar voice.

"Hello, Robert here."

"Guess what I found out today?"

"Oh hello there Fran. Nothing would surprise me. You are like a dog with a bone. Come on. Give."

Fran paused teasingly before stating,

"Mr William Elliott died in 1878 so what does that tell us?"

"So, little Charley boy lost out again. Poor little chap. Where do we go from here Fran ?"

"Well, how about the 1881 census again. Where was Frances then and who was with her? Not my idea but friend Amy suggested it may be a good move."

There was a subdued groan down the line before Robert agreed,

“Of course. I should have looked while I was down there. How daft can I be?”
There was silence for a moment before he spoke again,

“I’ll tell you what. I’ll go down there one day this week print off a copy for you, if I find her.”

“That would be great. Good hunting and we’ll see you soon. Bye Robert.”

**

Fran prepared a ham salad followed by blackberry and apple pie with fresh cream for Sunday lunch. It was a lovely warm late summer day and Leonard put out table and chairs on the patio and wine in the fridge in readiness for the guests.
Fran explained,

“Robert and I will no doubt go into a hunch when they come because I’m hoping he will have something to show me.”
Leonard’s face displayed a mock grimace as he replied,

“Tch. Not the ancients again for aperitifs! Will this never end? Up half the night buried in ancient history and now more artefacts for Sunday lunch.”
Fran was setting the table and threw a napkin at him in response,

"Go on with you. I think you're as excited as I am to find out more. Just hope he found something."

Raising her head to listen Fran said,

"Is that a car?"

There was some movement as the front door bell rang and a voice called,

"Are we in the right place for sherry?"

There stood Elizabeth with Robert waving a familiar looking paper.

Leonard moved forward with a huge grin to shake hands saying,

"I think you're about to satisfy somebody's curiosity Mr. Brentwood. May I suggest I pour the sherry and we all sit outside in the sun to study this very important, historic document together?"

When they were all settled and the sherry poured, Robert passed the paper to Fran,

"Because you suggested this I'm giving you the privilege of acquainting everybody with these facts.

Fran unfolded the foolscap page and read out loud,

"1881 census for Oldham.
Saunders Michael M 40 Head doctor of medicine
" Frances F 34 wife
" James M 5 son
Elliott Hannah F F 10 d in law
Elliott Charles W M 9 s in law

Fran finished reading and looked up at Robert incredulously.

"That is amazing. To actually see her there and with Charles too. What does it mean when it says 'd in law and s in law?'' I've not seen that before."

Robert traced the words she was pointing out and smiled,

"Ah! That simply means step daughter and son. It was often written that way. They were not his children but step children. What about James then?

"Yes. What about James! I'm just so dumbfounded at this. So much to take in. it doesn't clarify who the soldier was though does it."

"No it doesn't. Could have been either of the boys."

Fran gestured with her hands,

"I suppose there are some things we'll never know but to know so much is wonderful. Thank you Robert for making another trip."
Robert said thoughtfully,

"I believe I could find out which of the boys went into the army from military records. Next time I visit Kew I'll have a look." Pointing his finger at Fran he grinned,

"Until then you'll have to be patient, unless you beat me to it!"
Fran looked penitent but amused,

"I will try sir, but….."
Robert huffed,

"Now what?"

"Well I just wondered if Charles was with Frances and the danger was past, why didn't she reclaim young Robbie?"
Robert appealed to Leonard,

"Will this woman never be satisfied?"
Leonard shrugged comically saying,

"I very much doubt it until she has all the answers."
Fran chuckled and rising from her chair she turned to go inside,

"Now if everybody's had a top up, I think it's time for lunch."

**

Seated again outside with coffee, Leonard passed around the after dinner mint chocolates,

“Just to complement lunch before Fran brings on the buried treasure.”

Fran arrived on cue with a large package and laid it on the table.

“This is our hoard of jewels that belonged to our Gran Hannah Frances and probably to her mother, our joint ancestor Frances Saunders, lately Elliott, formerly Brentwood nee Brown, Phew. What a title!”

She was holding a carved box of beech-wood with a silver lock and key.

“Are you ready for this?”

There were nods of approval and impatient assents and Fran raised the lid to open the box. She lifted out a tray containing several rings in separate slots then took out a necklace of sparkling emeralds. Robert remarked,

“These are those green beads you remember Fran? They are beautiful and must be worth a fortune.”

Fran then lifted out a velvet box containing a sparkling necklace with matching bracelet and ear-rings.

Four pairs of eyes gazed at the collection with wonder. Robert was first to speak.

"My goodness! That is awesome. These must be the jewellery that Robert Brentwood bought Frances and she stored with Mr Weston."

"I think so." Fran picked up the emeralds and ran them through her fingers reverently as she mused.

"I wonder why she didn't sell them when she left Elliott."

Here Elizabeth intervened as she fondled the diamond bracelet.

"Perhaps she didn't need to."

Leonard voiced his thoughts,

"Maybe Brentwood left money with the solicitor as well as jewels. He sounded a sensible chap."

Fran said decidedly,

"Whatever the answer, we are left with all these valuables and as a family, need to decide what to do with them."

CHAPTER TWENTY

One hundred and thirty three years after Robert Brentwood married his Frances Brown, another Robert Brentwood was married to Charlotte Frances Smith on a sunny day in June. It was a simple wedding in the ancient village church where her Great, Great Great Grandfather was the Reverend Robert Brown. The bride looked radiant with a coronet of orange blossom and jasmine sitting on her russet gold curls. As she walked up the aisle on her father's arm, a short lace veil covered her face falling to her shoulders in soft folds. The elegant knee length, cream lace dress and jacket fitted her slender form to perfection. Sister in law Janet, her only maid of honour looked a picture in a knee length suit of palest lavender. With her silky dark hair dressed away from her face and falling down the nape of her neck she looked relaxed and happy. Her besotted husband watched adoringly as she followed a proud Leonard up the aisle, with Charlie on his arm.

The groom at her side, handsome in his grey suit, enhanced the vibrant beauty of the bride as the service united the two sides of a family and the sun caressed the two golden heads standing at the altar rail. The brightness streaming through the stained glass window struck fire in each green stone encircling the slender throat of the bride.

While the couple were signing the register, Fran played the haunting Nocturne on the old cello before herself witnessing the entry.

Later that evening, with the feast over, the principal actors left centre stage and drove off into the sunset to begin a new life together. Robert turned to Frances,

"So the threads of life's rich tapestry are drawn together and our families are close again. With your perception, I'm sure you think this is what our Frances had in mind."

"Well, I do think we have done something to atone for the misery she suffered and yes, I do feel she planned for posterity. I have never told anyone this although Charlie knows, but many times when I've been playing the cello, I've felt it pulsing with a power. Once or twice, I suppose when my mind was empty and most receptive, my fingers have been led without conscious thought."

"That's how you knew the nocturne?"

"Yes I think so but I often heard Gran Hannah hum the tune too."

"Perhaps now things have worked out the way she would have liked, our mutual Great Gran will rest in peace."

THE END

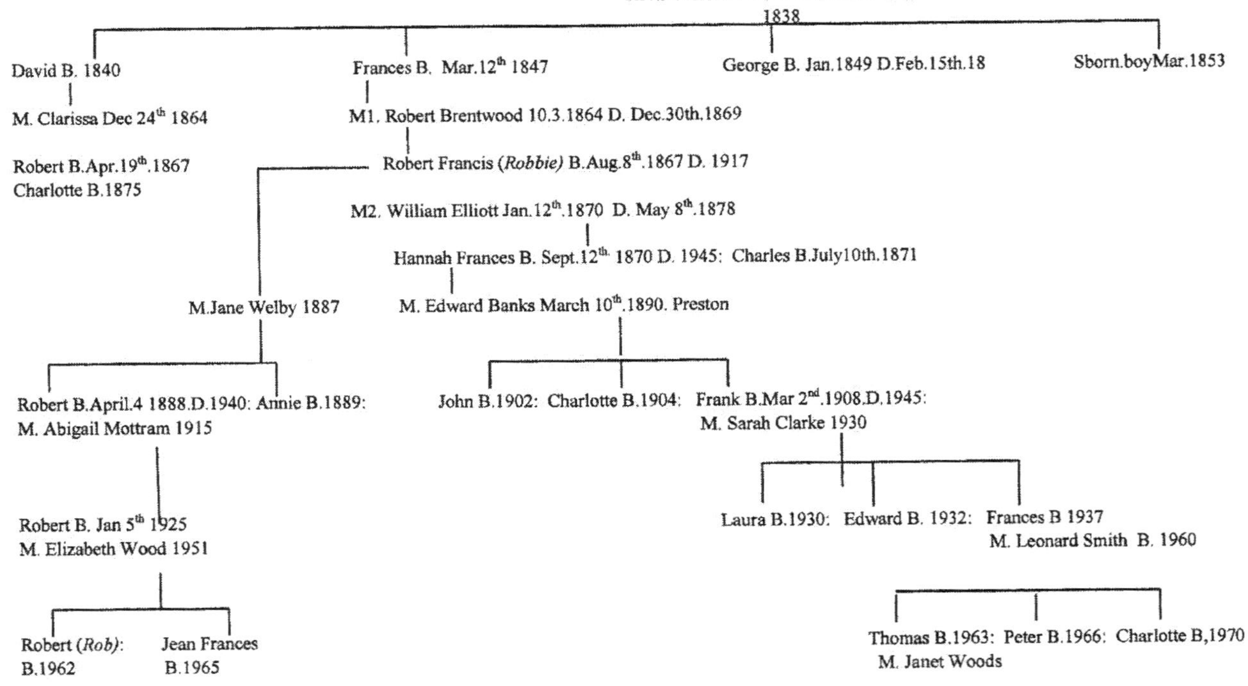
Rev.Robert Brown M Charlotte Davis
1838
David B. 1840
M. Clarissa Dec 24th 1864
Robert B.Apr.19th.1867
Charlotte B.1875
Frances B. Mar.12th 1847
M1. Robert Brentwood 10.3.1864 D. Dec.30th.1869
Robert Francis (Robbie) B.Aug.8th.1867 D. 1917
M2. William Elliott Jan.12th.1870 D. May 8th.1878
Hannah Frances B. Sept.12th. 1870 D. 1945: Charles B.July10th.1871
M. Edward Banks March 10th.1890. Preston
George B. Jan.1849 D.Feb.15th.18
Sborn.boyMar.1853
M.Jane Welby 1887
Robert B.April.4 1888.D.1940: Annie B.1889:
M. Abigail Mottram 1915
Robert B. Jan 5th 1925
M. Elizabeth Wood 1951
Robert (Rob):
B.1962
Jean Frances
B.1965
John B.1902: Charlotte B.1904: Frank B.Mar 2nd.1908.D.1945:
M. Sarah Clarke 1930
Laura B.1930: Edward B. 1932: Frances B 1937
M. Leonard Smith B. 1960
Thomas B.1963: Peter B.1966: Charlotte B,1970
M. Janet Woods

17326099R00119

Printed in Great Britain
by Amazon